AUDREY
ANONYMOUS

Kimberly Conn

Cover design concept by Jan Carlo Dela Cruz. Author photo by Johanna Cosby.

This book is dedicated to every mother who has had to put herself aside for the greater challenge of caring for her children. Being a mother is rarely glamorous and often comes without thanks or praise, but what you do for your children is immeasurable. You are immeasurable.

Without the support of my family and friends, this book would never have been possible. A debt of gratitude also goes to Meredith Shah for her time and brilliance in making Audrey's story presentable.

And for T.M. with love.

The opposite of addiction is not sobriety. It is human connection.

—Johann Hari

CHAPTER ONE

"Ow," I mumble, my cheeks stretched around invading fingers. The metallic taste of fresh blood trickles down my throat, and I gag. The hygienist quickly removes her hands.

"Your gums are so sensitive. Do you floss, Andrea?"

I frown and run my tongue across the back of my bottom teeth, which have been scraped, poked, and flossed until there can't possibly be any enamel left. I decide it's not worth reminding her for a third time that my name is Audrey.

"Daily," I tell her.

"Daily?"

"At least five times a week." I hate coming to the dentist for the same guilt trip and torture every six months. "Was that floss you were using waxed?" I don't add, *because it felt like barbed wire.*

"No, we really don't prefer it. You just may need to be a little more thorough. You've got to get up in there really good."

I wonder if dental hygienists ever need therapy, or if they release all their pent-up aggressions on unsuspecting patients.

"I noticed a good bit of staining on the backs of your teeth. Do you drink a lot of coffee?"

"None."

"Tea or dark sodas?"

"Rarely."

"Red wine?" Now she's getting somewhere.

"Occasionally," I say. I'm probably imagining the look of disapproval on her face. She can't possibly know whether or not I'm lying, and actually, I *do* only drink red wine occasionally. I used to drink it a lot, but wine only appeals to me late in the day. Pulling out a cork first thing in the morning seemed indecent, so when I started wanting a drink earlier in the day, I found out quickly that vodka was my new best friend. It mixes well with appropriate morning beverages like orange juice, is easy to disguise, doesn't linger on my breath, and rarely haunts me with a headache the next day. Plus, it's clear, so what stains is the hygienist even seeing? It's none of her business anyway.

When I finally break free from the dentist's office, my sole focus is finding my buzz. I'm antsy from missing my morning drink and try to remember where I last bought booze. I'm pretty sure it wasn't this side of town, so I drive to the nearest package store and load up.

People who work at liquor stores are the least judgmental people on earth. They see all kinds of people streaming in and out at all times of the day, buying every manner of alcohol for a hundred different reasons. I do, however, worry about running into someone I know as I leave with enough booze to keep me sane for a couple of weeks, so I try not to go to the same place too often.

I once had a fleeting thought that I could be an alcoholic but quickly dismissed it. Alcoholics have boozy smells seeping from their pores. They slur their words and stumble around. I smell like expensive shampoo and lavender hand cream and never allow myself to get completely drunk. Alcoholics alienate people and lose their jobs. I'm a full-time mom with two kids, and I volunteer at an animal shelter. Alcoholics don't—can't—function like I do.

It's remarkable to think how differently I used alcohol when I was younger. Before Enid was born, I was racing up the corporate ladder as a business consultant, working fourteen-hour days and power lunching with some of the smartest and most ambitious people I'd ever met. Back then I drank to make myself braver, louder, more confident and exciting. Alcohol energized me and helped me be the life of the party. I loved how it made me feel, and I'd be remiss if I didn't give a couple of glasses of wine some credit for landing more than one business deal and catching Stewart's attention on a project we worked on together. It's amazing what some liquid courage will make you ask for.

That seems like another life to me now, and my ambitions these days are limited to making it through a day without losing my mind. An MBA from Penn is no help with fits and tantrums and taught me nothing about walking on eggshells to keep both of my children from falling apart. Nobody else seems to notice the cracks and fissures threatening my own foundation, so now I use alcohol as an anesthetic. Since there are no business deals to be had (unless you count relentless negotiations with my teenage daughter), a constant buzz helps. It makes me feel evanescent, like I can almost disappear into the background. Sometimes that's exactly what I'd like to do.

I know what some people might say if they knew how much I drink, but I honestly think it makes me a better version of myself. Without it, I'd probably have run away from my life a long time ago. It may sound like the excuse of a woman whose drinking *is* a problem, but I know if I quit drinking tomorrow, I would not stay. It's awful to admit that, but it's true. I feel entirely alone when I'm at home with my family, and drinking numbs the part of my heart that knows how wrong it is to feel that way. In a sense, it solves my problems, or at least hides them from me for a while.

Every day I observe other women with their husbands and children, and I wonder if they are better people than I—kinder, smarter, more patient—or if they're a sheet and a half to the wind, just like me. I try hard not to reveal my discontent, however, because frankly, nobody cares about my problems.

Maybe every mother out there struggles to keep up the same charade. It could be the best-kept secret of all time: Ninety percent of suburban mothers are boozers! For every ten Starbucks cups you see in the carpool line, seven have been doctored with Kahlúa or Baileys. Wine isn't just for book clubs anymore! Sweet tea vodka is the preferred lunchtime beverage of the underappreciated southern stay-at-home mom.

As comforting as those thoughts might be, there is no sisterhood of tipsy mothers out there waiting to initiate me. You'd think every time I take a drink I would feel like a horrible person, but I don't—sometimes I feel like a hero for just sticking around. My family is, to say the least, a challenge.

CHAPTER TWO

Enid stomps into the kitchen like she does every day. I can hear her exasperated sigh outside the laundry room door as I hurry to return a bottle of vodka to its hiding place behind the books of carpet samples I never returned to the decorator. Enid is fourteen and has always been a difficult, emotional child, but she's been borderline multiple personality for the past couple of years. She's also a very wise and suspicious girl, so I unfold a stack of towels I just washed yesterday and shove them into the washing machine even though it's only six forty-five in the morning. I pick up my glass of Grey Goose and orange juice, take a long sip, and set it on the folding island before I face my daughter.

"I hope my skinny jeans are in that load of wash," she says, pointing, before I get both feet all the way into the kitchen.

"Did you bring your dirty laundry basket down yesterday?" I know the answer to this question, but I ask anyway.

"Since when do I have to do that? What do *you* do around here all day?" Enid sticks her bony hip out in a way that makes me want to strangle her.

"If you bring it down, it will get washed." I speak slowly to control both the volume and level of irritation in my voice. My once sweet little girl has transformed into an entitled, spoiled brat who seems to think she does enough every day just by gracing us with her presence when she feels like it. As if her existence alone is reason enough for me to buy her nice clothes and electronics and chauffer her to wherever her friends happen to be. God forbid she contributes something other than a crappy attitude.

"I have absolutely nothing else to wear!" Enid shrieks before glaring at me and stomping off to reconsider her wardrobe.

As a little girl, Enid was the child people couldn't walk past in public without commenting on how pretty she was. Lately, however, she has not been the least bit beautiful to me. She wears a constant sneer that occasionally morphs into a pout, and nothing makes her happy anymore except for her friends, who are generally surly and demanding, just like she is.

I retrieve my beverage from the laundry room just as Jacob pads into the kitchen in his pajamas.

"Morning, Jake!" I say. He looks at me and blinks a few times before climbing onto a stool at the counter where his breakfast waits. Breakfast is the same every day—plain, dry Cheerios, a tube of strawberry yogurt, and an apple juice box—and has been for nearly three years. Jacob will only drink from a straw, must use a particular bowl and spoon every day, and cannot do a single other thing until he's eaten breakfast. Weekends included. It's one of the many quirks of an autistic child.

I walk over and run my hand through his hair, which is a tangled mess from sleeping. Sometimes it doesn't bother him when I touch his head, but today his body goes rigid and he stops chewing until I pull my hand away. Jacob does not multitask, so me touching him while he's eating is probably too much stimulation at once.

I have a flash of memory from when I was very young. Every time my mother would walk past me, she would lightly scratch my scalp with her long fingernails, which were always painted red. It would tickle and give me goose bumps and make me giggle. Sometimes I think I even remember how she smelled. Every now and then I get a whiff of something sweet and perfumy that brings such a vivid memory of her it takes my breath away. It's one of the few things I truly remember about my mother, who died in a car accident along with my father when I was four.

My sister, Jane, and I went to live with our grandmother when our parents died. My grandmother, whom we called *Grandmother*, was elderly even then and didn't have the energy for young children. She treated us like adults from the beginning, and we did our best not to upset her. She never spoke about my parents, so for years I wondered if the memories I had of them were all in my imagination.

I have never been a physically affectionate person, perhaps because of the lack of affection shown to us by our grandmother, but I do sometimes pass by my children and touch them on the tops of their heads like my mother did to me. I always have a quick, fleeting memory of her, and wonder if Jacob and Enid will remember me that way when they are older. My fingernails are not long or colorful like my mother's, and my kids never giggle when I touch them, though, so probably not.

A loud thumping sound comes from the laundry room, so I leave Jake to his cereal and hurry to rearrange the towels that have piled up on one side of the washing machine and thrown it out of balance. When I come back out, I nearly trip over a heap of dirty clothes that has been dumped on the floor just outside the laundry room door. I cannot engage with Enid right now, so I kick the pile through the door and slam it shut, startling Jacob.

"Sorry, buddy," I say. "I didn't mean to close that so loud." He goes back to eating, and I'm grateful for his routine. I can always count on Jacob to stick to his schedule, and I'm careful to adhere to it faithfully as much as life allows. When he's done eating, he will go dress himself in the clothes we laid out last night. Jake will only wear things that are blue or green, will occasionally wear something with both colors, like blue *and* green stripes, but won't wear plaid. I made the mistake of buying him blue and green plaid shorts last year, but it was as if the lines going all different directions made the pattern too much for him, and he refused to wear them. I've learned since then to keep things simple, so solids are generally the safest bet. After he gets dressed, he will brush his teeth while humming the entire theme song to *Gilligan's Island,* and then he'll take his post next to the front door with his backpack strapped tightly to both shoulders until he sees his bus pull up in front of the house to take him to school.

A noise erupts outside the kitchen window, and Jake abandons his breakfast to jump down from the table and investigate the source. Reuben, the Yorkshire terrier next door, is barking up a storm. Jacob presses his nose against the glass and smiles. He likes Reuben. When he was younger, I would take him over to visit. Running his hands all over Reuben's fur soothed Jake, but one day I made the mistake of telling Reuben's owner, Mrs.

Speight, that Jacob is autistic, and she got it in her head that Jake might somehow be capable of hurting her dog. She began to pick Reuben up when we'd come over and make excuses for ending the visits quickly. It made me angry, and we never went back. I've harbored resentment toward my elderly neighbor ever since.

I stand behind my son and look out the window. Reuben is standing on the edge of the patio barking at a squirrel less than ten feet away from him. Most dogs would take off after the squirrel, but Reuben just barks. The squirrel, on the other hand, must be a regular in Mrs. Speight's yard and know it is safe from capture, because it stands still, staring Reuben down.

"Your bus will be here in twenty minutes," I say. I don't know if Jake understands the concept of time and minutes, but he at least recognizes this as a signal to get moving.

He waves to Reuben, though the dog is completely unaware he is being watched, and goes to his room to finish getting ready for school. I pack the lunch I made for Jake last night in his lunch box and put it inside his backpack. I used to put his lunch in a soft thermal bag, but about a month ago, his sandwich was squashed by the other stuff in his backpack, and he refused to eat it. This threw his whole day off course, and he came home hungry and foul, so I had to find a hard plastic lunch box. So far it's warded off unnecessary lunch-related meltdowns.

I finish my drink, a slight burn warming the back of my throat, and rinse my glass thoroughly before putting it in the dishwasher. I am very careful about leaving any trace of alcohol behind. I'm paranoid that Enid will drink from my glass by accident, and I'll have some serious explaining to do.

Enid comes back into the kitchen looking chipper, so I'm instantly on guard. She pours herself a small bowl of Special K with skim milk, which makes me sad because it's a reminder that she's weight conscious already. She's tiny and her features are so delicate she looks almost elfin at times, but nonetheless, peer pressure about food and body image issues has already begun. Stewart and I are both slender and so were our parents, so I tell her she has nothing to worry about, that good genes are on her side. My advice has a way of falling on deaf ears, however, the only opinions of worth to Enid being those of her fellow fourteen-year-olds. She has forbidden me to pack carbohydrates in her lunch, so I send turkey and cheese roll-ups, lots of fruit, and vegetable sticks with ranch dip. I don't know how she gets through a day without starving to death, but who am I to nag her when most days I take a liquid lunch?

"I've got some blueberries in the fridge if you want some on your flakes," I say, waiting for her to snap back at me that she has decided she hates blueberries and how could I not know that?

"That sounds good, actually," she says.

I get the container out and wash some berries for Enid. I set them on a paper towel beside her, and she thanks me. I am in for something. I feel it.

"Ready for your math test?" I ask, trying to keep things light.

"I think so," she says. "I studied pretty hard." She puts the berries on her cereal and picks up her cell phone to scroll through social media. I want to tell her to put it down and eat, but I hear Jacob coming down the stairs and look at the time. His bus will be here any minute.

"I'm going to walk your brother out."

"Okay," she mumbles, and as I leave the room, I hear the ding of her cell phone, indicating that communication with her friends has already begun at this early hour.

Jake stands at the front door, peering out through the heavy leaded glass to watch for his ride. I help hoist his blue backpack onto his shoulders, and he clips the little support belt around his waist. Jacob is the only child I've ever known who does this, but I know he will perch on the edge of the seat in the first row on the right side of the bus (the only place he will sit because he likes to be able to see out the front window), and he'll keep his backpack strapped to his body the entire ride to school.

When a yellow form appears through the window, I open the door and walk my son to the end of the driveway. Mr. Burns, the bus driver, stops and turns on the blinking lights before opening the door for Jacob.

"How's my favorite passenger today?" Mr. Burns asks as Jake climbs the stairs. Mr. Burns asks the same question of every child who gets on his bus, but it's one of the reasons I like him so much. It takes a certain kind of person with a certain kind of heart to drive a busload of special needs kids back and forth to school every day. He holds his hand up for a high five, which Jake returns, but with the back of his hand. It's an awkward motion, but Mr. Burns is one of the few people Jake doesn't mind touching.

Jake settles himself in the front of the bus, and Mr. Burns wishes me a good day before closing the door and driving down the street. As I walk back to the house, I say the same silent prayer I do every Monday through Friday that Jacob has a good day and that no surprises are in store for him.

Enid is not in the kitchen anymore when I return, and I can hear water running upstairs, so I relax. Surprisingly, her bowl is in the sink, though why the extra step to the dishwasher is so insurmountable, I'll never understand.

Several consecutive sounds chime from across the room, Enid's phone lighting up where she left it on the table. Curious about what could have so many sets of young fingers involved in a group text this morning, I listen carefully to make sure Enid is not on her way back down and take a look at her phone.

I press the home button to reveal several messages on the lock screen.

Beeyatch you are HILAR.
E didn't know u had it in u! What is k gonna do if she finds out?
You guys. Get me off the group text!! I'm over my f'ing limit . . .

I'm not so naive as to think teenage girls don't cuss or cause trouble, but it's never occurred to me before that Enid might be stirring anything up anywhere other than at home. She's never gotten in trouble at school or had a problem with a friend outside of school, but clearly she's involved with something I probably won't like. I've been thinking for months that I should install some kind of app on her phone that lets me see the texts she sends and receives, but I haven't done anything about it, plus now she has a passcode on her phone, so there's no subtle way to do it.

I try to think of who "*K*" could be, but Enid has at least three good friends whose names start with that letter, and none of them stand out to me as someone Enid might be mean to for any reason. I jump when I hear footsteps coming down the stairs and hurry to the other side of the kitchen so she won't know I've been spying.

When I turn around a moment later, Enid's phone is no longer on the table, and she is stuffing her carb-free lunch into her messenger bag.

"Can we leave a little early?" she asks, looking at her hands and picking at her cuticles. "I want to go by Mrs. Matthews's room before school to make sure I didn't miss anything on the study guide for the test."

She has never asked to be early to school before, but I give her the benefit of the doubt rather than listen to the voice in my head that tells me this has more to do with the texts and whatever she has gotten involved in than it does with math.

"Sure, give me a minute to get my shoes on and brush my teeth. I'll go straight to the shelter after I drop you off." She heads off toward the garage, where she will sit in my car waiting impatiently while I take five minutes to get ready. I pour some Red Bull and vodka into my favorite plastic travel cup with the big, swirly *A* on it and head to the car, knowing it will be a while before I can have another drink. When I get in the car, Enid barely glances up, her thumbs wildly tapping out a message to her people.

"Who's that?"

"Nobody."

"Can't be nobody," I tease, trying to catch a glance at her phone, wishing for a second we'd gotten her that ridiculously expensive one with the huge screen that she wanted instead of the smaller one we got free with our plan.

"Just some kids who couldn't figure out the last problem on the study guide. I'm telling them to meet me in

Mrs. Matthews's room, and we can figure it out together." She tosses her phone into her bag, and I'm shocked by how quickly she can come up with what I'm sure is a lie. We are silent for the rest of the drive, and I can hear her phone buzzing at the bottom of her bag the entire way to school. She must think I'm deaf or stupid. Probably both.

It's a relief when she gets out of the car, even though I know that whatever started this morning from a distance will now continue in person. Her phone has become an extension of her body recently, as if her heart will stop pumping blood if she is away from the thing for more than sixty seconds. At this point, a normal parent would take the phone and exercise their authority to demand the passcode and read the texts, but I just cannot handle the mushroom cloud of teen rage that will envelop my household without backup from another responsible adult. I don't know that I necessarily count my husband as a responsible adult since he's never home, but even if I did, Stewart won't be home from his current business trip for a couple more days, so I let it go for now, hoping that by the time Enid returns from school this afternoon, the entire situation has resolved itself.

CHAPTER THREE

D rop-off traffic is a nightmare, and it takes longer for me to get out of the parking lot than it did to get into it. When I finally reach the animal shelter where I volunteer, there is no time to spare before a truck pulls up, full of donations from the community. We unload old towels, bags of dog food, cleaning supplies, and stacks of old newspapers for lining the enclosures. My back and shoulders ache by the time we are done, and I'm grateful to find my purse and cup sitting exactly where I left them.

The animals here are so pitiful, and it's hard to look past their sad, pleading eyes. I don't know the story behind every one of them, but I'd like to think that being here is better than wherever they were before. The people who work and volunteer here are so good to the animals that it has to be better than the alternative, even if they are eventually put down. At least they've experienced some concern and dignity along the way.

I'm in the lobby talking to Frank, the shelter supervisor, when a battered minivan pulls right up to the front door. A haggard-looking woman climbs out, and my stomach churns. It's obvious she's not here to pick out a pet, so she must be here to dump one. Frank sees her, too, and sighs.

We push through the door and into the bright sunlight, where the woman has opened the back of her van and is wrestling with something, cursing loudly as she yanks on a chewed-up leash.

"Can I help you?" Frank asks, hurrying to assist the woman.

"You can get this goddamned horse out of the car is what you can help me with," she snaps.

Frank takes hold of the leash and climbs partway into the van, calmly coaxing the animal forward. I'm still wondering about the horse comment when Frank emerges, followed by the largest—and ugliest—dog I have ever seen.

"Good Lord," I gasp as the woman slams the tailgate shut and heads back for the driver's side door.

"Um, excuse me. Ma'am? Are you surrendering this animal?" Frank gives the dog a scratch behind his ears.

The dog looks at him with grateful eyes, as if Frank is doing him a favor.

"You bet I am. I got four kids and my mother-in-law under my roof. I don't need an oversize furball to take care of, too."

Frank bristles. "I need you to come in for a moment so we can get the background and health information on the dog." He hands me the leash, and the dog follows me obediently into the shelter lobby.

"I didn't know this was going to be complicated," the woman says, exasperated, as she reluctantly enters the room with Frank right behind her.

"What's his name?" I ask, trying to lighten the mood.

"Budweiser," she says. I suppress a chuckle and wonder for a second if she gets through her days the same way I do. I decide to call him Bud.

Bud stands nervously by the desk while his owner gives Frank as much information as she can muster, which isn't much.

"Age?"

"Probably a yearish."

"Veterinary history?"

"None."

"So he hasn't been vaccinated?"

"Nope."

"Are height and weight known?"

Said with an annoyed eye roll, "Big and heavy."

"Is there any other reason why you are giving him up? Is he aggressive? Has he bitten anyone?"

I look at the dog, whose long, matted fur is hanging over his eyes. He looks embarrassed, like he understands the questions and wonders why they are being asked in the first place, as if it's not perfectly clear who the asshole in the room is.

The woman shakes her head. "I got him from a guy selling puppies in the Walmart parking lot. Thought my kids would like having a dog, just didn't know he was gonna be so damn big. I ain't got that kind of room."

"Thank you for your help," Frank says respectfully. I know he tries hard not to judge people who abandon animals and always says not everyone is equipped to care for a pet. The woman turns and leaves the building without asking a single question about what will happen to Bud now. Frank and I stare at the enormous dog standing in the middle of the room.

"I don't know where we're going to put him," he says. He shakes his head and looks at me. "Have you had lunch yet?"

"No, but it can wait. Why don't I help you figure this one out?"

Bud is the calmest, sweetest animal I've ever been around. He waits patiently with his leash tethered to a table while Frank and I try to find an enclosure large enough to fit him and seems completely unfazed by the noise of other, curious dogs. The problem with Bud is multifaceted. He appears to be an Irish wolfhound, already ridiculously big, and Frank says that if he's only a year old, he could grow for several more months. Plus, who is going to come in here and pick out a beast like this over a cute, cuddly puppy? He has never received treatment from a vet, so getting him his shots will be an expense, too. I can tell Frank is contemplating the logic of starting the process of vaccinations when the likelihood is that Bud will be euthanized by the end of next week.

"He deserves a chance," I say to Frank, though he hasn't asked my opinion.

Frank nods, deep grooves forming in the space between his eyebrows. "Audrey, do you mind cleaning him up? He's filthy, and nobody's going to see any potential in a dog that looks like he's spent his life in the dirt. If I had to guess, he probably has fleas, too."

Bud follows me to the bath area. I tell him to sit and he looks at me blankly, but when I gently push down on his rear end, he seems to understand and drops his rump to the floor. I wet him down, and he shakes a little but doesn't try to run. I can't see any fleas jumping on his coat, but I give him a good scrub with special shampoo just to be sure and comb through his long, tangled fur, cutting out some of the more serious mats with scissors. Bud seems to enjoy the attention and, except for soaking me with a massive shake after I rinse him, is very cooperative. He looks like a different dog when I return him to Frank, who has decided to use an exercise run to house Bud for the time being.

"Wow, that's an improvement," he says, giving Bud a pat. "Maybe he's got a ten percent chance to live now." As soon as he says it, he winces because there's a lot of sad truth there. He sighs. "I'm going to get him started with vaccinations. You just never know."

I grin, but my hope is short-lived when one of the other volunteers comes hurrying down the corridor. "Audrey, you've got a phone call. It's your son's school."

Like any normal parent, my first thought is that Jacob is hurt or sick. But then like any parent of a special child, that thought is immediately followed by one imagining the many things Jacob could have *done* to warrant a phone call. I pick up the receiver in the office.

"This is Audrey Anderson."

"Hi, Audrey, it's Vivian Marshall. I'm sorry to bother you at work." Vivian is the principal, so that pretty much rules out Jacob being sick.

"I'm not working, just volunteering. Is Jacob okay?"

"He's fine, but he's locked himself in a bathroom and won't come out. It's creating quite a disturbance. I thought you could help."

I am uncertain why calling me is necessary. "Can you send someone under the stall to unlock the door?"

"It's not that kind of bathroom. The children were in the school library, and Jacob got into a conflict with another student over a book. Mrs. Lewis tried to separate them, but Jacob had the book in his possession and ran into the handicapped bathroom and locked the big, heavy door."

"Surely there's a way the janitor can get him out. Kids must get locked in there all the time."

"He tried, but the little keyhole on the outside knob has something shoved into it, so the jimmy key won't go in. The next option is to take the door off the hinges, but we thought we'd try you first to see if you could come talk him into coming out."

"Are you sure he's okay?" I ask, imagining a million things that might happen to Jacob while he's locked behind that big, heavy door.

"We can hear him in there singing or something. I don't think he's crying. I've heard him cry before, and it's . . . well . . . louder."

She's right. When Jacob cries, everyone in a mile radius knows it. I hang up the phone and grab my purse and cup. I let Frank know I'm leaving and give our newest tenant a quick rub. He seems to get cuter every time I look at him, or maybe he's just growing on me. Maybe he'll get lucky.

⇒┼┼⇐

When I get to Jacob's school, several adults are gathered outside the door to the library restroom. Vivian Marshall apologizes profusely for the inconvenience, as if this isn't just another normal day for Jake and me.

I press my ear to the door and listen. I can hear his voice faintly, and it does sound like he's humming. I can't tell if it's the *Gilligan's Island* song, but at least I know he's not in distress.

I knock. "Jacob, it's Mom. Can you come out, please?"

He stops humming, but the door does not open. "Jacob, you need to unlock the door. You're making everyone worry."

I wait. Nothing.

"Jake, bring the book out, and Mommy will take you to the bookstore to pick out the exact same book so you can have it at home." It's silent for a minute and I'm about to panic, but then the doorknob starts to turn.

The crowd behind me exhales as Jacob exits the bathroom clutching the book. I extract it from his hands. It's a *Clifford the Big Red Dog* book. He has seen the cartoon on TV but has never expressed an interest in print books. His teacher thinks there is too much going on between the words on the page and the pictures and that it frustrates him. The fact that he has latched on to a book is interesting.

"Thank you, Audrey!" Mrs. Marshall exhales. "We didn't want to take the door off unless we absolutely had to." She lowers her voice. "Power tools tend to scare the children."

I think of all the things the teachers and administrators have to worry about every day in this building full of special needs kids. Each one has his or her own

Kimberly Conn

quirks and fears, and I feel bad that I wondered what the big deal was in taking the door off the hinges to get my child out. A whole series of new problems could have been created if a drill had been fired up. I never even stopped to consider how that might have affected Jacob on the other side of the door. He would have been terrified.

"If it's okay, I think I'll just go ahead and take Jacob home with me." I give Mrs. Marshall the book, take Jacob by the hand, and walk to his classroom to collect his backpack and lunch box. I apologize to Mrs. Lewis for the trouble Jake caused, wave to his five classmates, and we leave the building.

"Ready to go home?" I ask, not really expecting an answer.

"Book," Jacob says. I did promise to buy him the book when I was trying to coax him out of the bathroom.

"That's right, the book about the big dog?"

"Big dog," Jake parrots.

An idea hits me as I lean in to buckle him into his seat. "Jake, want to go *see* a big dog? A really big dog?"

He starts nodding so enthusiastically that his forehead slams into mine, making my eyes water. When I can see straight again, I look at my son, who is covering his forehead with his hand but not shrieking like I would expect after a collision like that.

"Big dog," Jake says again. I need a drink.

The shelter is unusually quiet when we walk in. A lot of the volunteers have left for the day, but Frank is in his office.

"I didn't expect to see you back today," he says when I tap on his open door.

"I hope it's okay that I brought Jacob back to meet Bud."

"Everything all right at school?"

"As all right as usual," I say with a forced smile. My buzz has completely worn off, and I'm getting tired and agitated.

"You're not worried Bud will scare him?" Frank asks. He's been witness to a couple of major Jacob meltdowns but still graciously allows me to bring him to visit once in a while.

"If he freaks out, I promise to carry him straight to the car. I don't want the animals getting wound up. It's so quiet right now."

Frank gets out of his chair. "Isn't it? Melissa thinks Bud's arrival is having some kind of magical calming effect on the whole bunch. I don't know if I agree with her theory, but whatever the reason, I'll take it. It's a nice change."

We walk to the run where Bud is lying in the back corner. He's still clean and combed, and when he sees us approach, he stands up and ambles over to the door of the enclosure.

Jake gasps when he sees the size of the dog walking toward him. For a second I think I've made a mistake bringing him, but when they are almost nose to nose, Jake sticks his hand through the bars, and Bud licks it with his long, slobbery tongue. Jake squeals with delight, eliciting a few barks from the other dogs nearby, but does not move his hand away. Bud licks it one more time and then takes a couple of clunky steps so that Jake's hand rests on his back.

"Big dog," Jacob says, his stubby fingers stroking Bud's fur.

When I bring myself to tell Jake it's time to leave, he pitches a fit, wrapping his fingers tightly around the metal bars of the run door. I pry his hands away, and when I do, he turns them on me, slapping at my face and pulling my hair angrily. I finally pin his arms to his sides and haul him, spitting and screeching, out to the car. Jacob is small for an eight-year-old and weighs less than fifty pounds, but when he gets like this, he may as well be a three-hundred-pound gorilla. I manage to wrestle him into his car seat and fasten his seat belt, then climb into the driver's seat and catch my breath.

I check myself in the rearview mirror, push the hair out of my face, and wipe the sweat from my forehead. My cheek is bleeding where Jake must have caught me with a fingernail. I grab a tissue and dab at it, the sting of the cut not nearly as bad as the sting of embarrassment I feel after the scene Jake just made.

Maybe it was terrible judgment on my part to bring him to the shelter today, but strangely enough, I'd do it again just to see the peace and calm that came over Jake while he was petting Bud. Frank might not be too keen on me bringing him again anytime soon, but maybe if I ask Mrs. Speight nicely and assure her Jake will be gentle, she'll let us start coming to visit Reuben again. I suggest it to Jacob as I drive, but all he says is, "Big dog." He can be pretty obsessive about things.

When we get home, I settle Jake in front of the television and pour myself a generous shot of vodka. I don't bother to mix it with anything, knowing I'll have to do that when Enid gets home. My hands shake as I lift the glass to my lips, but before long, I'm feeling like myself again. I don't know when I started thinking that way, that feeling like myself means having booze actively working its way through my bloodstream. Having no alcohol in my system makes me feel . . . less like me.

A gentle yank on the hem of my shirt startles me, and I spin around to see Jacob standing right behind me. The child usually moves like a herd of elephants, but this time I didn't hear him approach.

"Aren't you watching your show?" I ask.

He holds the remote control out to me. This is a request to channel surf, so I bring my glass and sit beside him searching the eight million cable channels for something he'll like. I scroll right past *SpongeBob SquarePants* because the voices all sound like yelling and Jake gets agitated by it. Normally he likes *Tom and Jerry* on low volume, but today he makes the noise that means no, so I keep going.

I sip and scroll and finally hit pay dirt. *Marmaduke* is showing on one of the movie channels, and Jake is immediately bouncing and giggling at the sight of two dogs half floating, half swimming through an underground sewer system. There is some drama as rescue crews attempt to save them, but all Jake seems to see is the dogs. If the action gets too loud, I can mute the TV and I doubt he'd notice, except that right now the dogs are "talking" to each other and Jacob is enthralled.

I lean back and put my feet up, enjoying having a happy child, though I know the moment will be over all too soon. I hit record on the remote so that we will at least have part of the movie to watch again, and I make a mental note to order the DVD.

At times like this, I wonder why it is that I struggle to keep it together so much of the time. I know other parents with autistic children, plenty with emotional, angry teenagers, and even one or two with both, like me. The difference is that they make it look easy to the point of heroism, whereas I celebrate making it through another hour with a cocktail—or more accurately, it's the cocktail that ensures I *will* make it through another hour.

I look at Jacob, his mouth open and tongue lolling out as he watches the movie end happily. I wish I could just enjoy him and his uniqueness, but the things that make him so unique also make him a constant source of worry and dread. I want to be a good mother to him, but so much of the time, I just don't know how. I tip my glass to my lips and realize it's empty. A good mother would remain on the couch, snuggled up to her son, but my son doesn't snuggle, and I head back to the kitchen to refill my drink.

CHAPTER FOUR

Late in the evening, I have reclaimed my perfect high. Jacob is watching the last part of *Marmaduke* for what might be the hundredth time, Enid is upstairs doing homework after a rather incident-free return from school, and I've decided not to bring up the text thing for now. I've convinced myself that good parents should stop meddling in their kids' lives and let them work out their own issues.

Earlier, I cooked the last box of macaroni and cheese for Jake's dinner, which he ate at his usual spot at the counter. Enid took yogurt and fruit to her room, and I got out some cheese and crackers to go with the bottle of wine I opened.

My family has not eaten a meal at a table together since Jacob was four years old. Not for Christmas, Easter, or even Thanksgiving. I remember the last time we did eat together as a family so well because it was a horrible experience and a real turning point for me. We had gone out to a restaurant—not even a particularly nice one—with the kids, and Jacob had a nuclear meltdown when the well-meaning waiter made a happy face out of ketchup on his plate next to the French fries. We were still in the early stages of trying to understand and manage an autistic child and were completely unprepared for the situation.

I used my napkin to try to wipe the ketchup from his plate while he screamed as if he had been set on fire. When every trace of the ketchup was gone, I gave it back to him, but he picked up the plate and threw it, showering Enid with food before the plate hit the ground and shattered. I scrambled to the floor to pick up the pieces of broken porcelain while uttering words of apology to the waitstaff and other customers nearby. Enid was in tears and Jake kept on screaming, and Stewart *just sat there staring at us.* As if the whole situation had nothing to do with him, like we were somebody else's family.

I picked Jacob up and took Enid by the hand, hissing at Stewart to pay the bill as I fled to the car. I buckled my children into their seats and stood outside the car as a light rain started to fall, thinking about how easy it would be to just walk away. To leave them in the car, where Stewart would find them in a few minutes, and run. As unprepared as I was with just thirty dollars in my wallet and damp clothes on my back, it would have been easier than staying, knowing as I did that this kind of thing would happen again and again.

I remember how it felt as the realization set in that I could not leave. I took a few deep breaths and joined my children in the car. Jacob was still shaking, but his screaming had quieted to a whimper. Enid's face, streaked with tears, looked relieved to see me, as if she knew what I'd been thinking as I stood out in the rain. We sat in silence for nearly thirty more minutes before Stewart finally got in the car and drove us home without saying a word. I never asked, but I have a feeling he stayed at the table and finished his dinner in peace, grateful that the rest of us weren't making a scene anymore. God forbid his life change just because mine had.

To this day, I imagine him sitting alone at the restaurant, calmly taking his time to eat his meal while the rest of us sat in the car. I never addressed his lack of response to the situation, and he certainly didn't ask how he could have been more helpful. We went home, I poured myself a drink—quickly followed by another—and that was the last time we had dinner as a family. It was also when I began to understand how well alcohol helped me deal with those situations.

Mealtime now consists of me feeding the kids in shifts and then eating when I get around to it. Once in a while when Stewart is around, I might actually cook a proper dinner for the two of us, but family dinner just doesn't exist in our home anymore.

Jacob walks into the kitchen as I take a sip of Cabernet and stares at me.

"What's up, Jake?" I ask.

"Book," he says.

I groan, having completely forgotten, but knowing there will be no happy ending tonight unless we go get that book. Thank goodness Barnes & Noble is still open. I holler up to Enid to let her know we are going out, and put Jacob in the car.

In my rush to get this errand done and get back to my wine, I throw my car into reverse, realizing too late that I failed to open the overhead garage door. I slam on the brakes, but not until after I've backed into a wall of paneled wood, the sound of metal crunching and wood splintering a sickening combination. I curse under my breath as Jake whimpers, pull the car forward again, and climb out to assess the damage. The tailgate of my SUV is dented, though still intact, but I've banged up the garage door pretty badly.

Afraid to hit the automatic open button on the garage remote, I am able to manually raise the door. I write this accident off as being in a hurry, not being tipsy, and hop back into my car, backing out more carefully this time. I just hope everything can be repaired before Stewart gets back from his business trip to New York.

Twenty minutes later, I am cursing Barnes & Noble. I've come in for one *Clifford the Big Red Dog* book, but there are at least a dozen different Clifford books all nestled together cozily on a shelf. Knowing I'll never make it out of here quietly with just one, I buy them all.

On the drive home, I look over my shoulder a couple of times to see how Jake is doing in the back seat. The shopping bag full of picture books is clutched to his chest, and he's looking out the window with the most serene expression on his face. I wish I could know what he's thinking. Or that a bag of picture books could make me as content as Jacob looks right now.

I make Jacob take a bath before he can take the books out of the bag, and thankfully he complies with only a minor fuss. Enid is locked in her room, and I knock lightly on her door to let her know we're back. She does not respond at first so I knock harder, eliciting an irritated, "*What?*"

"We're back," I tell her.

"Duh," she says. Her voice sounds raspy.

"You okay?"

"Why wouldn't I be?" she asks, which means she's not. My daughter may seem alien to me lately, but one thing I know for sure is when she's trying to pretend nothing is bothering her.

"I'll be downstairs if you need me," I say and start to walk away before turning back and tapping on her door again. "I forgot to ask how your math test went."

"Fine, I guess." Her voice is definitely raspy, like it gets after she cries or yells, both things she often does when communicating with me. We have not had any sort of confrontational exchange this evening, so something else must be wrong.

"Did you get your grade back?"

"No."

"Okay," I say. "Can I at least see your face?"

"I'm doing homework. I'll come down in a little while."

I don't like the nagging feeling I keep getting where Enid is concerned, but I don't want to start a war. Maybe she'll come talk to me later if I don't push.

"I love you," I force myself to say. I don't say it enough lately, because Enid has been such a challenge to *like*. There is no response from behind the door.

I extract Jacob from the tub and settle him in his bed surrounded by his new books before returning to the kitchen, where the rest of my bottle of Cabernet awaits. I have just finished pouring myself another glass when the house phone rings. It's usually Stewart this time of night, so I answer it quickly without looking at caller ID.

"Hello?"

"Who's this?" a young female voice asks on the other end of the line.

"You called me. Who is *this*?"

"Um, is Enid home?"

"Are you a friend of hers?" She still has not identified herself. Good phone manners are nonexistent these days.

"Can I just talk to her real quick?" the girl asks, sounding unjustifiably annoyed by my question.

I hold the phone out to read the caller ID, but it's a wireless number, so no name is displayed.

"She's upstairs doing homework right now, but I'd be happy to take a message and have her call you back. It might be tomorrow, though. It's pretty late."

"That's okay," the voice says, and she quickly hangs up. I thought she might do that. If this were about schoolwork, any child would have easily said as much. I scribble the number from caller ID onto a piece of paper and slip it into my pocket just as Enid walks into the kitchen.

"Was that Dad?" she asks.

"No, actually, it was for you."

"Who was it?"

"I don't know. She wouldn't tell me, and she didn't leave a message."

"Did you check caller ID?" Her eyes are huge.

"It was a cell phone. Are you expecting someone to call?"

"No," she says defiantly, "but why didn't you come get me?"

"You were locked in your room and didn't seem interested in talking to anyone."

She makes a noise, the one that is meant to make me feel like even more of a parental failure than I already do. The one where air angrily leaves her body through every opening she has. The one where she sounds inconvenienced, disgusted, and fed up all at the same time. The sound *I* should be making right now, not her.

"You don't have the right to screen my calls."

"Oh yes, I do," I say.

"What if it was important?" She stomps her foot like a toddler.

"She had every opportunity to tell me if it were important, but she wouldn't even tell me her name!" My brain has begun its tirade by way of my mouth, but my heart is willing it to shut up before I push Enid farther away. "It makes me think you and your friends are up to no good." Now I've done it. I've tipped her off to my suspicions and pissed her off royally with one sentence.

My daughter looks at me as if I've just slapped her, but I can tell by the look on her face that I'm not far from the truth.

"What have you done, Enid?"

"Nothing!"

"Has a friend of yours done something and dragged you into it?" For a split second she looks thoughtful, and

I think she might be about to tell me what's going on, but in a flash, her expression reverts to anger again, and she snatches the phone from the counter.

She hits the button to bring up the last caller, and I lunge at her to grab the phone. I inadvertently knock the phone from her hands and it goes flying, landing on the hardwood floor with a clatter. Enid holds her hand to her chest, tears brimming in her eyes.

"You hit me!" she screams. I freeze. I did not hit her. My hand hit the phone receiver, but it never even *touched* her.

"Are you kidding me?" I ask, but Enid has already fled the kitchen and is running up the stairs to her bedroom. I holler after her. "I want your cell phone in my hand in the next two minutes, Enid!"

I wonder what Jacob thinks about the yelling. He's probably curled up in his bed with the covers pulled over his head. I pick up my wineglass, empty it in three gulps, and head for the stairs to check on Jake. When I get to his room, he is not in his bed, which sends me into a minor panic. I look around frantically, checking under the bed and in the closet. It's not unusual for me to yell at his sister, but if he got upset about it, there's no telling what he might do to make the noise go away.

I call his name a couple of times, trying to sound calm, but he's unlikely to answer. I notice the door into his bathroom is cracked, which he usually doesn't like. He prefers doors to be all the way open or all the way closed. I push on the door carefully in case he's right behind it on the other side. The bathroom is dark, but in the shadows I make out the shape of my son standing on the lid of the toilet, looking out the window. I exhale.

"Jake, what are you doing?" I ask, grateful to have found him quickly. He's not hiding and doesn't appear to be upset.

He points out the window into the darkness outside. I move behind him to see better, and follow his finger to the little spot next door where Mrs. Speight's porch light illuminates her yard. She is standing in her bathrobe watching over Reuben while he takes his last pee break of the day, and Jacob has been observing silently from his bathroom window. I wonder how he knew they were out there and if he's done this before, perhaps often.

We stand together and watch until our neighbors retire for the night, and I help Jacob off the toilet and into his bed. It's not until I pull his door closed that I remember demanding Enid's phone. Prepared for the next battle, I take a deep breath and knock with authority on her door. She answers it almost immediately with her phone in her hand.

"I'm sorry I got mad," she says, handing it to me.

"Me too." My cheeks feel warm and my heart is beating quickly, so I take a deep breath before I speak. "I'll be honest with you, Enid, I'm a little worried. This morning you left your phone in the kitchen, and I wasn't trying to meddle, but I noticed you got a bunch of texts all at once." She doesn't look at me.

"Then you wanted to go to school early, even though you said last night you were totally ready for your test, so that seemed a little strange. Earlier tonight it sounded like you were crying, and then you got a call from someone who refused to identify herself, and you were desperate to know who it was. I think you might be able to understand why I'm a little uneasy. I don't want to assume you're doing anything wrong, but my gut tells me not to ignore these concerns."

Enid finally looks at me, her eyes welling up with tears. "I didn't want to tell you, but I'm in a fight with Kara."

"Kara?"

"Abbott," she clarifies. I bristle. I don't care for Kara Abbott's mother.

"What about?"

"She was saying mean things about Jake." The tears start rolling down her cheeks, and I can tell that at least this part is true. Nothing makes her angrier than when people are cruel to her brother, and she's not such a good actress that she can manufacture these very real tears. What's surprising is that Kara Abbott is the one talking ugly about Jacob. Her younger brother has Asperger's syndrome, so you'd think she'd be more sensitive.

"Did you retaliate?" I ask, remembering the texts this morning about Enid being mean and what "K" will do when she finds out what Enid did. I know girls can be dramatic and spiteful, but I tend to think Enid is nice to pretty much everyone but me.

"Kind of." She turns around and sits on her unmade bed. Her curtains have been closed all day, and it smells like stale vanilla as I follow her farther into her room.

"Kind of?"

"She was talking about how her brother is 'smart autistic,' like this boy Clay in our science class who's a genius, and then said that Jake is the dumb kind of autistic, like he's mentally retarded or something."

The words are arrows through my heart. Sometimes I think I've become numb to how other people see Jacob, but that's only when my mind and body are numb from alcohol. I can't deflect the hurt myself, so how can I expect Enid to let it roll off?

"So what did you do?"

She looks at the floor. "I told a boy she has a crush on that she likes him."

"Well, that doesn't sound awful. Especially if he likes her back."

She shakes her head and snorts. "He doesn't like her. He doesn't even know she exists! He's a *senior.*"

"A senior?"

She nods.

"I didn't know you talked to seniors. Do I know him?"

"No, how would you? I don't really know him, either, but he accepted my follow request on Instagram, and I posted it to his feed."

This is one of the many things I hate about social media. Kids might only have a handful of good friends in real life, but they can have hundreds through these outlets and not even know most of them.

"Why would a high school senior you don't know approve your follow request?" I don't mean to undermine Enid, but thankfully she doesn't take offense.

"It's all about numbers," she says. I cringe at that answer. Kids think their value can be measured by the number of people reading the stupid, inane stuff they post on the internet. It's ridiculous.

"So you posted *on his page* that Kara likes him?"

Another nod.

"Does she know?"

"No, and she won't."

"Enid, kids talk. Your friends who were texting you all morning will tell someone at some point. It will get back to her. It always does."

"There's no proof it was me," she says.

"How? Don't you post with your name and picture?" It's no secret that I check her page once in a while. That was the rule for letting her get an account in the first place.

"I didn't post from my account. Hannah and I made a spam account, and we used a picture of her cousin as the profile."

I like this less and less every second. "That's sneaky and probably illegal. You can't pretend to be someone else, Enid. Can you take the post down?"

"Yeah."

"Then do it. Delete the account, too. All that can be traced, you know."

She stares straight ahead, and I can tell she's thinking about something else.

"I still don't get it," I say. "This didn't just happen today, because your friends were reacting to it at breakfast. Why didn't you get upset about it before now? Maybe Kara decided to pick on Jake to get back at *you*."

"She doesn't know," Enid says confidently.

"Well, end it. I know you want to stick up for your brother, and I appreciate that more than you know, but of all people, Kara should be more considerate."

"Thomas is autistic lite," she says under her breath.

"Excuse me?"

"Her brother has Asperger's. He's not *that* autistic. He's super smart and a little weird, but he'll go to college and move out one day. Jake never will. Kara wasn't really wrong about that, but it still makes me so mad!" Tears start streaming down her face again, and I can barely breathe. I've thought those exact same things before, inside my own head. I've had my own issues with Kara's mother in the past because she lumps us into one category—*mothers of autistic children*—but I resent her because I feel like my struggles with Jacob are so much greater than her struggles with Thomas. I would give my left arm if Jacob could be described as "super smart and a little weird." Her son goes to public school, for crying out loud!

But for my daughter's sake and my own, I say, "That's not fair. Thomas has his own challenges—they're just different from Jake's. Kara had no right to say that to you, but you need to let it roll off. You need to take down that fake account *today* and be the bigger person."

Enid sighs. "*Okay.*"

"Jake is lucky to have a sister who cares so much," I say, laying my hand on hers. She yanks her hand out from under mine and tucks it under her leg.

"He's just so vulnerable, Mom."

"I know." I walk to the door with her phone still in my hand. "I know."

I tell her to turn out her lights soon, and I head back to the kitchen, where I pour what's left of the wine into my glass. I would love to drink myself into oblivion right now, but something about this whole thing with Enid isn't sitting right with me, and I can't cloud my thoughts any further.

I turn her phone over in my hands and press the home button, fully expecting the passcode screen to light up and mock me. Instead, I see the word *Hello.* I swipe the screen with a finger and am prompted to set up an account. Unbelievable. That little sneak reset her phone. I can only imagine the smugness she must have felt when she handed it to me. It probably compares to the smugness I feel now as I restore the entire thing from the cloud. She hasn't outsmarted me yet.

An hour later my eyes are crossed from staring at the tiny screen, but I still haven't figured out the alias Enid used to post on that senior's feed since I have no clue who the boy is to begin with. I should have asked, but it's a little late for that now. I scour Enid's Instagram and even Kara Abbott's until my head pounds, but I am no closer to answers. I finally toss the phone on my nightstand and fall asleep on top of the comforter, the last thing I think as I drift off being that Stewart never called tonight.

CHAPTER FIVE

I t's a quiet morning in the house. I don't plan to say anything to Enid about her phone, because really, what's the point? It's better to just not let her know that for now I'm a step ahead of her, and fighting with her this morning is something I cannot handle. I woke up with a killer headache, so I'm sipping a vodka and Red Bull to try to get me going. My goal today is just to survive Enid.

Jake brings some of his new books down to breakfast, and I read them aloud while he eats his Cheerios and yogurt. He listens attentively, squeezing his eyes shut tight and grunting—his version of laughing—when Clifford follows his little girl, Emily Elizabeth, on her summer vacation. Jacob doesn't find many things funny, so when he does, it's a small reminder that there's an eight-year-old boy in there. When he abruptly leaves the table to finish getting ready for school, I stay there, soaking in the peace and quiet for a few extra minutes.

Enid slinks into the room, and I notice with some annoyance that she's not wearing the skinny jeans she demanded I wash yesterday. She doesn't make eye contact with me while she pours her flakes and skim milk, so I clear Jacob's dishes and tidy the kitchen in silence before meeting him at the front door.

"Are you taking your new books to school?"

He nods almost imperceptibly, his eyes focused out the window.

"Will you share your books with your friends?" He furrows his brow, and I know it's a request he's unlikely to fulfill. Jacob doesn't really have friends. His class is very small, and he doesn't interact with the other kids voluntarily. The fact that he fought over a book yesterday is kind of remarkable, because it actually required interaction.

I can relate, because I don't have many friends, either. When Enid was little, I had more friends than I can now fathom—women with whom I organized playgroups, traded off babysitting in exchange for "free time," and tried to outdo with more elaborate birthday parties than the ones before—but as Jacob became a toddler and his differences became more obvious, my support network started to wane. He can be a hard kid to spend time around and makes a lot of people uncomfortable, so we started getting fewer and fewer invitations to play and socialize. The ones we did get I turned down because taking Jacob to playdates became more a source of trouble and embarrassment for me than they were worth.

For a short time we had a small network of other autistic kids and their parents whom we got together with, but I started to feel as if I was forcing Jacob into situations that just weren't natural for him. Some of those kids, like Thomas Abbott, progressed and went on to "regular" schools, but at some point it became obvious that Jacob wasn't making the same progress. There were days I wondered if his development had stopped altogether, which made me wonder what I was doing wrong. It became easier to just manage Jacob on my own. Being a mother seemed like a competition most of the time, and I felt like with Jake, I was always coming in last.

I look at my son as he stands at the front door and remember the conversation I had with Enid last night. Jacob is the kind of autistic you can tell just by observing him, so people often judge him immediately. I personally don't feel judged as much as I feel pitied, which pisses me off. I wish things would change, for him and for me, but this is my reality, and it's not going to change while I'm on this earth. I will never be an empty nester, taking extravagant vacations and visiting my grandchildren.

I'll always be a caregiver to my son and forever wallow in my own self-pity.

Jacob looks up at me, and I quickly wipe away the tears that have started rolling down my cheeks. Sunlight coming through the glass in the door reflects in his green eyes, making them almost twinkle. I force a smile at him, and he turns his attention back to watching for the bus.

Jake's psychologist once said to think of the word "spectrum" like the light that is dispersed by a prism. "The light comes out in a beautiful array of colors like a rainbow, and sometimes it just takes your breath away," he said. He's right. I look at Jacob now, at the uniqueness and vulnerability that being *on the spectrum* brings, and sometimes I can see that it *is* beautiful, but as far as it taking my breath away, I frequently feel like I literally can't breathe with the weight and responsibility of it.

The bus comes into view, and we walk out in silence. As he's about to climb the steps, I want to stop him and tell him that I love him, but I honestly don't know if Jacob understands or feels love, and the certainty I have that I will never get a response back is painful. Lately I've started to wonder the same thing about myself, whether I really understand or feel love anymore, and I stand, mute, as he boards and the bus pulls away.

I stop in the foyer on my way back into the house to determine Enid's location. Her muffled voice is coming from her room, which means she must be on the phone. My stomach growls and I feel light-headed all of a sudden, so I head into the empty kitchen to eat some breakfast and finish my drink. My glass is not next to the sink where I thought I left it, but I quickly spot it on the island, where I must have set it down on my way to walk Jake out. I toast an English muffin and smear peanut butter on it before hurrying to my room to get ready to take Enid to school.

There's a knock on my bathroom door while I'm brushing my teeth, and I invite Enid in through a mouthful of foam. She has on a full face of makeup, which is usually limited to a conservative amount of blush and lip gloss. She definitely has on eyeliner today, and I think even some sort of foundation, because her skin looks flawless . . . except for the mascara that is applied so heavily she looks like she has two tarantulas perched on her face.

"Wow. You look so . . . grown-up," I say after spitting.

She smiles and leans casually against my vanity. "Thanks."

"I think you might have overdone the mascara a bit, though." I quickly follow with, "Everything else looks great," to seem supportive, even though I'm not particularly happy that she looks eighteen right now.

She leans in front of me to check herself in the mirror. She reeks of berry-scented body spray, and I have to take a step back.

"Ick," she says, wiping at her lashes. "I'm not very good at that part. How do I get it off?"

I get some cotton balls and makeup remover out of my vanity and help her exterminate her eyes, using a little of my own concealer to touch up where I've wiped hers off.

"Much better, thanks," she says, admiring her reflection.

"Sure," I say. "You probably don't have the best lighting in your room for putting on makeup. Maybe we can get you a mirror with a light so you can tell how much you're putting on."

"Okay," Enid says. "Hey, I came to tell you that Hannah's sister is going to drive me to school today." Hannah is Enid's best friend, and her older sister is a very responsible upperclassman, but since Hannah's the one who helped Enid with the fake Instagram account, I hesitate.

"We're going to take down that post in the car on the way," Enid adds quickly.

"Oh, okay, then. If you don't mind my asking, what's with the makeup and perfume?"

She shrugs. "I guess I just wanted to look nice today." Her expression darkens a little, a reminder of the emotional firestorm that's constantly simmering beneath the surface. "Is that okay?"

I don't want to risk an angry outburst right now, so I don't push any further. "Of course, you're just growing up so fast." I change the subject. "When are you getting picked up?"

"Like, now. I'm going to go grab my stuff." She turns to leave.

"Enid?"

"What, Mom?"

"You're doing the right thing, taking the account down. Ninth graders shouldn't be tangled up with twelfth graders. You'll be in over your head before you know it."

"Got it, Aud," she says, waving a hand dismissively and breezing out the door.

Aud? There is not enough alcohol on planet Earth to get me through the next few years until she goes to college. I can't even think that far ahead, because sometimes it's hard to imagine we'll ever make it.

I walk Enid out to meet her ride, which clearly annoys her. I want to make eye contact with Hannah, so I lean in as Enid climbs into the back seat. Hannah looks at me sheepishly from the passenger seat, which I take as an indication of remorse about what the girls did. Hannah and Enid have been friends since third grade, and Hannah's always been nice to be around. She's the only one of Enid's friends who makes an effort to speak to Jacob, while the others just glance at him like a minor annoyance and then disappear to Enid's room for hours at a time. I'm relieved to see the shy, guilty look on Hannah's face and want to hug her at the same time to thank her for backing Enid up in her effort to protect Jake. I wave as the car backs out of the driveway and feel a bit lighter walking back into the house, until I remember that Stewart hasn't called in two days.

When Enid was born, Stewart and I agreed that I should stay home. It was an easy decision at the time—money was certainly not an issue, and it seemed to be what all our friends were doing. Smart, accomplished women were becoming smart, accomplished moms. The enthusiasm and determination I had put into my job as a consultant was easily redirected into motherhood. Our home was a perfectly organized, childproof environment, where I could throw my energy into filling my baby girl's mind with letters, numbers, shapes, colors, and my undivided attention. Stewart began to withdraw, but his excuse to be an arm's-length father was always that Enid was a girl. He claimed to not have the first idea about how to care for or entertain her, and I was more than happy to be the one who was better at being a parent. For once I wasn't competing with Stewart to be the best.

Being a mom to Enid was not much different for me than being in the corporate world. Our schedule was planned down to the half hour, music classes followed by arts and craft workshops and visits to story time at the local bookstore. Enid was a vibrant, chatty toddler, dressed in perfectly coordinating outfits. She knew her alphabet long before she started preschool, and we spent countless hours at the zoo and children's museum. My daughter was a perfect little darling except for the tantrums she was prone to throwing. I was quick to write those off as exhaustion from our busy schedule or low blood sugar, quickly cured by a nap or carefully selected organic snack. As far as I was concerned, I was winning at being a mom.

When I got pregnant a second time, Enid was already in school. I was her room mother and volunteered to organize class activities and scheduled engaging playdates with other girls her age, but she was growing up quickly and didn't need me as much. I had visions of a new baby infusing my life with twice the purpose, and I was ready for it all over again. When my obstetrician told me I was having a boy, Stewart took a sudden, renewed interest in the baby. He would lay his head on my growing belly and talk to our son about sports. Toy footballs and tiny jerseys started appearing in our home, and I felt as though I had gotten Stewart back after a long absence. He even started giving Enid, who was seven by then and quite independent, more attention.

We had a great first year . . . almost. It wasn't until Jacob was about nine months old that we realized he wasn't doing some of the things Enid had done at the same age. He never giggled and rarely cried, wasn't crawling yet, and hadn't started with the *da da da, ma ma ma* babbling we'd found so entertaining when Enid was a baby. Our pediatrician told us not to worry, that every child is different and develops at a different pace. Our friends told us how lucky we were to have a quiet baby who wasn't climbing all over the furniture and getting into things. We tried to enjoy him, but we were worried and impatient, praying things would change.

When he finally crawled and then—amazingly, almost overnight—walked, we were so relieved we ignored the other things that weren't improving. He still wasn't talking, never seemed to look directly at us, and shied away from other kids when we were around them. Someone suggested that perhaps a hearing problem was the culprit, but that hearing issues are easy to diagnose and treat. I desperately wanted to believe this, but when we took him for testing, his hearing turned out to be fine. Not only that, but he started responding to sudden, loud sounds by throwing fits and shrieking hysterically. My quiet, content son was neither of those things anymore, and by the time Jake was two, we knew something was very wrong.

During this time, Stewart decided to take up golf, as if he needed an excuse to make himself physically scarce for several hours at a time. He became an avoider and started to distance himself from the kids again, particularly when either of them was having what he referred to as "a moment." *"Enid is having one of her moments. She needs some space." "I just don't know what to do when Jacob is having a moment. He's so unreasonable. What's the* matter *with him?"* It was as if when something happened that Stewart couldn't control, he checked out.

When we got the official diagnosis that Jacob was autistic, Stewart started working longer hours and throwing himself into his projects, his "commitment to his work" earning him VP status and almost constant travel on behalf of his company. These days I think he finds excuses to travel more frequently and stays away longer than he needs to just so he doesn't have to be here. I hate him for it and envy him for it all at the same time.

The phone in the kitchen startles me when it rings, and I answer it quickly, assuming it will finally be Stewart. I'm surprised when I hear my sister's voice on the other end.

Jane and I don't speak very often. Even after losing our parents, I never felt very close to her. She was always a bossy older sister, more than making up for my lack of mother and our grandmother's indifference. I think that's part of what motivated me to be so successful in school. When I graduated summa cum laude and went on to business school, I thought I'd make Jane proud, but she acted as though I abandoned her. She never finished college and was married before I finished high school. She was divorced twice before I even met Stewart and has had a string of unsavory men in and out of her life ever since.

We might talk every few months, but I haven't seen her in nearly five years. She flew in for Thanksgiving with her third or fourth husband, Leo, whom we hadn't met before. He was a complete loser, treated my sister like garbage, and—we realized after they left—stole all the cash from my purse, Stewart's wallet, and Enid's piggy bank. I called Jane when we noticed the missing money, but she got angry with *me*, made excuses for Leo, and ended up sending a check as her way of apologizing. She's not married to Leo anymore, and the last time I talked to her, she mentioned some guy named Mark or Mike or something like that. They live in Montana, which is far enough away that I hope to never meet him. I've already decided he's a loser, too.

"Jane," I say, the surprise in my voice undeniable.

"Hi, Audrey. Am I catching you at a bad time?" Jane's voice is gravelly, and I'm reminded of her awful smoking habit. Our grandmother smoked, too, so I feel as though my entire childhood was lived in a cloud of tobacco smoke. I can almost smell the stale stink of decades of Marlboro Lights through the phone, and I cringe.

"Not at all. Is everything okay?" On the rare occasions Jane calls, I always think she's calling to tell me she has cancer or something. It's awful, but it wouldn't surprise me.

Jane coughs and sighs. "Can't I just call without something being the matter?"

"Actually, that's the preferred way," I say, trying to sound lighthearted. "How are you?"

"Good. I have a new job. I started managing the stable on a ranch about a month ago. I really like it." Jane had been working in a doctor's office for a while but complained that they wouldn't let her smoke during office hours because she came back inside smelling like cigarettes. She's had more jobs than she's had husbands, but I guess it's good she likes this one.

"They let you smoke at the stable?" I think about all the wood and hay and wonder if that's a good idea.

"Well, I'm trying to quit, so whether they do or not isn't going to be an issue. I like being around the horses. They make me feel really calm. There's a dog named Hank who lives at the ranch next door, and he comes to hang out most days. He's good company."

"I can imagine you taking care of horses, actually, and I agree that animals are good company . . . better than people sometimes."

Jane laughs and coughs again.

"I'm glad you're quitting," I say. "Those things are terrible for you."

"Thanks for the information," she says sarcastically. There's a long silence, and I start to get uncomfortable. I'm about to invent an errand as an excuse to get off the phone when she speaks again. "How's Enid?"

"She's fine. So is Jacob."

"Teenage years going okay?"

"As okay as teenage years go. You know, she's emotional and temperamental, and I'm a complete idiot. The usual."

"God, what we must have put Grandmother through!" Jane chuckles.

"If I was awful to anyone, it was probably you," I tell her. "You raised me more than Grandmother did."

"She was a peach," Jane says, so quietly I almost don't hear it. "But really, is school going okay for Enid? I know high school is a big adjustment for a lot of girls. How are her grades and friends and whatnot?"

Annoyance pricks at me. Jane doesn't have kids and rarely concerns herself with mine. She sent Jacob the entire *Magic Treehouse* collection for Christmas because she read somewhere they were great for kids his age. She *knows* he's not like other kids his age. To this day, the books are still in a box in the attic. I should donate them but haven't gotten around to it yet.

"She's got straight A's, as expected," I say. "She's brilliant, you know that. Friends are fine, all gossip and giggles. Why do you ask?"

Jane hesitates. "Well, I ask only because I saw a comment she made on Instagram that made me wonder if she might be having trouble adjusting. I'm sure it's nothing."

"You're on Instagram?"

"Yeah, trying to get with the times."

"What *comment* did Enid make that was so alarming?" I can't hide my irritation, and Jane backs off.

"It wasn't *alarming*, Audrey; it just caught my attention. I'm sure it was nothing. She said something about how she could relate to Holden Caulfield. I didn't know who he was, so I looked him up."

"He's the main character in *Catcher in the Rye*," I quickly interject to show my sister how much I know. "That's a classic novel, Jane."

She lets out an exasperated sound. "I know that *now*," she says. "Sorry I'm not as well read as my Ivy League sister, but it seems like a pretty heavy book for a girl her age, and what I read about it says there's some language and a lot of references to sex and hookers and stuff like that."

"Oh, so you read the *CliffsNotes* and assume you can interpret what Enid's comment meant? He was a teenage boy, Jane. She's a teenage girl. All teenagers are full of woe and drama. I can assure you Enid is not having sex and is certainly not planning on becoming a hooker."

"Fine," Jane says curtly. "Forget I mentioned it."

"Look," I say as my cell phone starts to ring, "I've got to run."

"Sure, okay. Tell the kids Aunt Jane says hello."

"I will," I lie and hang up, hoping I don't have to talk to my sister again anytime soon.

I reach for my cell phone and check the screen this time before answering. When I see Stewart's name lighting up, I don't know whether to be relieved or annoyed. Already upset by Jane, I snap a grouchy *"Hello"* into the phone.

"Morning," he says. He sounds tired.

"I was wondering if we were going to hear from you again," I say.

"Come on, Audrey. What's that supposed to mean?"

"You haven't called in two days. As if nothing bad could possibly happen at our house in that amount of time." It pisses me off that he doesn't even seem to have noticed that we haven't spoken in forty-eight hours. It's as if he forgets we're even here when his big, important job is right in front of him.

"I'm sorry, with the time change . . ."

"Time change? You're in New York, Stewart. The last time I checked, it's in the same time zone as Atlanta."

"Well, I ended up having to fly to Japan last night, so it's a *thirteen-hour* time difference."

"You're in Japan? What the hell?"

"Calm down, Audrey, it was last-minute, and the company plane was being held for me. I barely made it. I was asked to lead the negotiations at a meeting in Tokyo tomorrow morning. The VP from the New York office was supposed to do it, but his mother died. Since I was already in New York, he passed the baton to me. If we get the bid, it would be the biggest project our firm has ever had." He sounds giddy, which irritates me further. I will myself to be happy for him, but I just can't.

"Did something happen at home?" he asks when I don't respond. "You sound really stressed."

"Nothing for *you* to worry about," I tell him. "Just some girl drama. And Jake locked himself in the bathroom at school. I had to go talk him out."

"Sounds like another normal day in the Anderson house." His remark is infuriating, and I almost ask him how he would know what a normal day in our house is like when he's rarely here, but I don't have the energy for a full-blown argument.

"Where are you?" he asks when I don't respond.

"Home."

"Are you working today?" I think he calls my volunteer job "work" to make me feel better. It doesn't.

"No." I don't feel like adding banal details for Stewart's benefit.

"You should go get your hair and nails done."

I look at my fingers, the splitting nails and overgrown cuticles. Stewart doesn't know me very well at all. A day at the salon would feel good until the second I got home, and then it would be as though it never happened. My money is better spent on Grey Goose.

"Maybe," I say, but I won't.

"Well, I better get to bed. I didn't get any sleep on the plane because I was going over the proposal."

"What time is it there?"

"Ten-thirty. P.M.," he adds, and I roll my eyes. I've been to Tokyo before, though it seems like a lifetime ago. I know it's P.M. I hear Stewart yawn loudly. I used to find it so endearing the way he yawned, stretching his arms way out and balling up his fists like a child. Now it's irritating, and I want to shake the image from my head and tell him to grow up.

"Get to bed, then," I say. I don't wish him luck.

"I'll call you tomorrow, I promise. Bye, Audrey." I wait a second before I hang up, not sure what exactly I'm waiting for. He doesn't tell me he loves me anymore. He used to say it every time he walked out the door or before he hung up the phone. Now I can't remember the last time I heard him say it to me or to the kids. He ends the call, and I toss my phone onto the counter. I feel like I need another drink . . . or two.

I don't know how Stewart and I got to this point. How did decisions we made together drive us so far apart? We are practically strangers, even though we once lived such parallel lives. Our paths have taken such a drastic turn away from each other that I feel we don't even know each other anymore. He's pitching billion- dollar projects in Asia, and I'm sitting at my kitchen table wondering when I gave my life away, and if my children are to blame.

I spend most of the next hour trying to get repairs scheduled for the garage door and my car. I'm going to have to have the garage door completely replaced and stained, which means I will have to have the other door restained to match. It's going to cost a fortune, but I don't want to involve the insurance company. Thankfully, they can get started on it tomorrow.

I take my drink to my room, shower, then roam the house trying to invent something to do. I end up in Enid's room, sitting on her bed, looking around at the clutter that represents her life. I don't know how much time has passed when I hear my phone ring. It's still in the kitchen, so I hurry to answer it, nearly slipping as I descend the stairs, and grab it, the words "Jacob School" lighting up on my home screen. *Not again.*

"Audrey." Mrs. Marshall exhales when I finally answer. "I'm sorry to bother you two days in a row."

"What is it today?" I ask, bracing myself.

"I'm afraid Jacob has locked himself inside the bathroom again. Are you available to help coax him out? You know I'd hate to have to resort to those power tools."

I sigh and look at the clock. "I'll be there in twenty minutes." She thanks me and I promise to hurry, but I sit for a minute and take a deep breath before collecting my purse and walking out to the driveway, where my dented car is parked outside the broken garage door.

I drive, feeling more buzzed than usual, suddenly regretting the third drink I had before ten o'clock. My brain feels impaired, and I have to think carefully about where I'm going. I drive cautiously in the general direction of the school, but when my cell phone rings again, rattling the cupholder it's sitting in, I flinch and nearly sideswipe a parked car. I ignore it, sure it's Vivian Marshall calling again to ask what's taking me so long.

Knowing it will cost me a few more minutes, I pull into a fast-food drive-through and order a black coffee and a large cup of ice. I pour the coffee over the ice so it cools off enough to drink it quickly, and by the time I get to Jake's school, I feel somewhat centered again.

I sign in at the office and hurry down the corridor to the library. Mrs. Marshall is standing outside the same bathroom as yesterday, looking more worried and disheveled than usual.

"Thank you for coming . . . *again*. I hope this doesn't become a daily thing. It's been a challenging day, even for this school." She says it "*skewel*," as she pushes a wisp of gray hair from her forehead. "Holler if you need me. I have a meeting with a parent that should have started ten minutes ago." She hurries out the door at nearly a sprint, on to her next crisis. Vivian Marshall's daily uniform consists of pants and flat-soled shoes. I think about the principals at the schools Enid has attended, dressed in pencil skirts and high heels that click as they walk purposefully down the tiled hallways. Mrs. Marshall's job is so much more physical and draining, and she never *walks* anywhere. I don't know how she does it.

I turn and knock gently on the bathroom door, aware of the librarian's disapproving eyes on me.

"Jake? It's Mom." Nothing.

"Jacob, I need you to come out. You can't keep doing this."

I turn to the librarian. "Excuse me, but do you know why he was in the library again today? His class was just here yesterday."

She smiles thinly, not showing her teeth. "I was teaching a lesson on the difference between fiction and nonfiction books. As they were lining up to go back to class, your son ran in there and locked the door."

My son. I want to remind her that he has a name and ask why in God's name she needed to teach Jake the difference between fiction and nonfiction, because he won't understand or even care, but I don't. Some of the other kids *are* capable of understanding, and just because I don't know how much Jacob understands or knows doesn't mean he isn't absorbing any information. He just can't convey what he knows in any way I can comprehend.

I knock a second time and press my ear to the door. "Jake, if you don't come out right now, I'm going to ask Mr. Dent to come take the door off with his drill. The drill will be very loud, and it will scare you. I'm counting to ten."

Before I get to three, the door opens, and Jake jumps into my arms with his hands over his ears. I scoop him up and carry him to a nearby table, where I take his chin gently in my hand so I can see his face. He closes his eyes so he doesn't have to look at me.

"Why did you lock yourself in the bathroom again? Was it because of a book?"

He breathes out through his mouth. "Big dog."

I wonder if he has wrangled himself into this situation for a second time because he thinks he will be rewarded with more Clifford books, but then he opens his eyes, and they lock on to mine, and he says, "Butt." For a moment I think he might be calling me a name, but when he sticks his tongue out and starts to pant, I understand. He means *Bud*.

This is huge. Not only because he's looking at me—directly at me in a way that he only does once in a great while—but also because I think I understand his intentions. He purposely locked himself in the bathroom so that I would come get him and take him to see Bud like I did yesterday. It's manipulative and sneaky, but it means he has thought about it in some way. Jacob made a plan.

I don't even bother with the inner debate about giving in to his tantrums and know that this may mean he'll never make it through another full day at school again, but I don't care. We practically run to his classroom to get his things, but we're almost giddy by the time we reach the car, Jacob's sweaty, sticky hand tight in mine.

CHAPTER SIX

I'm worried that Frank won't approve of Jacob coming
with me to the shelter two days in a row, and I'm prepared to beg for forgiveness after we've visited Bud, but
it's not necessary. The assistant supervisor is in Frank's
office looking frazzled.

"Is Frank here?" I ask, standing in front of Jacob so
she might not notice him.

"No. He had a heart attack early this morning and
was rushed to the hospital."

I feel like all the air has been sucked out of my body.
"What? Is he okay?"

"I don't know. Apparently it was a big one. He's having bypass surgery now. Honestly, I'm so overwhelmed I
don't know where to start."

"Is there anything I can do? For you or for Frank?"

"Say a prayer for both of us." She forces a smile. "Let me get through some of this paperwork, and I'll let you know. Thanks."

"I'm not on the schedule today, but my son wanted to visit Bud. Is that okay?"

"Bud?"

"The wolfhound that was dropped off yesterday."

She presses her palm to her forehead. "Oh God. I forgot about him. We need that run, Audrey. If he's not gone by the end of this week . . ."

"Frank said he was going to start his shots, and we got him looking so much better. He's a special case."

"What's special about him?" she asks.

"I can't explain it," I tell her. "He just is, and Frank thought so, too. You should have seen the mess he was yesterday, but he's got the sweetest eyes, and he's so calm."

"Aren't they all a mess when they come in? If it weren't for those sad puppy eyes, none of them would ever leave here. Don't even look at me like that. I can't put time into just one dog when now I've got to run this entire shelter on my own." She looks down at the piles of paper on Frank's desk. I take this as a signal she's done talking to me.

I walk Jacob down to the run where Bud is being kept. He is lying down, a gigantic heap of fur, but when he sees us, he hoists himself off the ground and trots over to say hello. Jake sticks his fingers through the metal bars and gives Bud a scratch, muttering sounds of adoration under his breath. Bud sits, his tail swishing giant arcs across the concrete floor.

The two of them seem to have the exact same expression on their very different faces: joy. I can't allow this animal to be put down, and with Frank gone, there is no other option.

"Jake, want to bring Bud home with us?"

Jacob shuffles his feet excitedly and begins to cry. Afraid that his arm is stuck in the gate or that, God forbid, Bud has nipped at him, I pull it out gently and inspect it. "Are you okay?"

"Ma," he says, shaking free of my grasp, and I can see he is smiling through his tears. "Butt!"

I feel something deep within me bubble up to the surface. It feels like progress, like hope, which to me is almost elation. Jacob has communicated more in the past hour than he has in entire months recently, not so much in words as in meaning. Jake will not leave Bud's side, so I hurry to the office and tell the assistant supervisor that we want to adopt Budweiser.

Same-day adoption is unusual at our shelter, but since Bud is taking up space in a needed run and because I was screened before I started volunteering here, they gladly make an exception. I sign the contract and pay the adoption fee, convincing Jacob to leave with me for an hour so we can go to the pet store to buy all the things we need to have for Bud before we can bring him home.

Jake picks out some toys, sticking with his preferred blue and green color scheme. I talk to a store employee about dog food for an Irish wolfhound and load sixty pounds of kibble into the cart. We choose a dog bed large enough for a small horse and the biggest doggie playpen they have in stock, in case Bud isn't housebroken.

When we return to the shelter, the back of my SUV is so packed with dog gear that I have to load Bud into the middle row with Jacob. Jake squeals with delight, making my ears ring all the way home, but Bud doesn't seem to mind at all.

At home, we take Bud out to the backyard to let him pee, but he seems confused and nervous, shaking a bit and not going more than a step away from either of us. Jacob explores Bud's entire body with curious hands, peeking inside his ears, lifting up his tail, rubbing his belly. I have yet to hear Bud make a sound, but when Mrs. Speight lets Reuben out into her yard and the little dog makes a beeline for the fence, barking furiously, I brace myself.

Bud doesn't bark back, instead moving between the yapping dog and Jacob, as if to protect him. Mrs. Speight comes out onto her patio to shush Reuben, and I wave at her casually over the fence.

"What's he barking at?" she asks, walking toward me.

"Jake's here," I say as she stands on tiptoe to peek over the wood slats.

"Oh my," she gasps, pulling her cardigan tightly around her. "What on God's green earth is that?"

"We got a dog," I say cheerfully. "We brought him home from the shelter today. He was going to be euthanized pretty soon, I'm afraid."

"So you rescued it?" she asks, her tone contradicting her choice of words.

"We did." Jacob is now kneeling on the grass next to Bud, nuzzling him behind the ears like a mother dog. I'm so happy I'm not even bothered by the disgusted look on Mrs. Speight's face.

"Is it aggressive? It looks like it could swallow Reuben in one bite."

"*His* name is Bud, and he wouldn't harm a fly." Mrs. Speight frowns. "He doesn't even seem to be all that curious about Reuben. Reuben came tearing at the fence barking like crazy, and Bud barely moved."

"Hm. Well, I hope he doesn't decide to become more interested. He's frightening looking."

"I don't think you need to worry." *Screw you, old lady,* I think to myself. I leave her standing at the fence and take Bud and Jacob inside so our dog can investigate his new home. I'm too pleased with Jake's obvious excitement to be mad for long. We have a dog! Jake is happy! Stewart is going to freak out.

I'm so smitten with Bud—and more importantly the bond he seems to have forged already with Jacob—that

I nearly forget that I made a ridiculous spur-of-the-moment decision without consulting half of my family. He's gentle and calm, and when Jake isn't lying all over him, he stands nicely by the door to the deck and waits to be let out into the yard.

Enid brings me hurtling back to reality when she walks through the door after school.

"What is that disgusting thing?" She tosses her backpack on the floor, frozen, mouth gaping open.

"Our new dog," I say from my position on the living room rug, where I've been sitting watching my son and his new best friend for an hour. I haven't felt the need for a drink since we've been home—this euphoria is something I want to really feel. "And be nice. He's really sweet."

"That's not a dog," Enid says, frowning. "It's, like, a camel."

"He *is* a dog. His name is Bud. It's actually short for Budweiser, if you can believe it."

Enid shoots me a strange look before turning her attention back to Bud. "I can't believe you brought that thing into our house. It's hideous."

"He's *not*," I say sharply. "Watch for five minutes. He's huge, and I know he's strange-looking, but seriously, E. Watch."

Enid stands at a distance, but when I look at her a minute later, her eyes are wide, and her mouth is turned up at the corners. She takes a step closer to listen to Jacob, who is whispering into Bud's ear. Bud raises a bushy eyebrow, as if mulling over whatever Jake is telling him.

"What's he saying?" Enid whispers, coming two more steps closer.

"I have no idea," I say, "but it doesn't really matter. He's been like this all afternoon."

Enid finally sits down on the rug next to me but keeps her voice low. "How did this happen?"

"He was dumped at the shelter yesterday. You wouldn't believe the shape he was in, filthy, neglected, and just—sad. But he's so sweet and gentle. My supervisor, Frank, had a heart attack today, and I realized that if everyone had the same initial reaction to Bud that you did just now, he'd be put down in just a few days without Frank there to help people see the good in him."

I'm overcome with sadness for Frank and hope he is able to make a full recovery and return to the shelter. Bud rests his head on the floor between his front paws, and Jacob presses a cheek to his belly as if it's a giant pillow made just for him.

I tell Enid about the past two days with Jake and the school bathroom, and she laughs at the thought of her little brother doing it on purpose again today. I have not been this close physically to both of my children at the same time in ages, and it feels good. Enid and I never sit around like this and talk, and right now I feel like we are behaving like a normal family. For the first time in a long time, I don't feel lonely in my own home.

"So he's really staying?" Enid squats down and crawls over to stroke Bud's stringy gray fur. Jake giggles, listening to the strange gurgling noises coming from Bud's stomach.

"I think the bond has already been solidified," I say. "I'll admit I didn't think very hard about it before signing the papers, but I think this could be really good for Jake. For all of us."

Enid nods and tousles Jacob's hair. "Do you love your new doggie, Jakey?"

Jake turns his head and grins at his sister. "Butt," he says, and we all laugh. My eyes fill up without warning, and my laughter mixes with tears.

"Are you okay, Mom?" Enid looks at me with concern.

"I'm great," I assure her. "I'm happy we could give Bud a family." I'm also happy that Bud has, for the time being, brought my family back together.

Late in the evening, we are all still in the same room. Enid is doing her homework on the couch, looking up often from her studies to watch her brother. I have not had a drink since before I picked Jake up at school, but as things have settled down, I've begun to miss the buzz, and my forehead aches a little.

Bud carefully slides himself out from under Jacob and positions himself by the door. Enid gets up from the couch, and we all follow him outside, as if he is an alien life-form we are conducting scientific observations of. Bud is fascinating and lovely in his strangeness, and we have completely taken ownership of this animal.

The sun is low behind the trees, casting strips of orange light onto the grass in our backyard. Bud seems more comfortable now and wanders around, inspecting his environment, which I'm guessing is vastly different from the place he started his day yesterday.

Jacob follows him closely but steps back quickly when Bud stops and squats, depositing the largest pile of poop I've ever seen on my lawn. Enid gags. Jake stares, rapt. I laugh out loud, feeling renewed in a way I would not have imagined a day ago.

The phone inside the house rings, and Enid runs to answer it. For a brief moment I think about the phone call for her last night, but when she comes back outside with the phone to her ear, there is nothing secretive or private about her actions. She speaks animatedly to whoever is on the other end, talking about Bud and giggling. She hands me the receiver and bounces over to Jacob and Bud, who has found a patch of waning sunlight to lie down in.

"Hello?" I say, as it dawns on me whose voice I am about to hear.

"We seriously have a dog?" I can't tell if Stewart is surprised, amused, or angry. "Is this some kind of payback for me going to Japan without telling you first?"

I can't help but laugh. I was so angry with Stewart this morning, but Bud has been such a wonderful distraction that none of my usual worries have entered my mind for hours. "No, it's actually not, and if you can believe it, it was cheaper than a day at the salon. I'm sorry I made such a spontaneous decision—a big one—without consulting you. I wish you could see this . . . can you FaceTime me from there?"

"I think so," he says. "Let me hang up and try your cell."

I run into the house to get my cell phone and hurry back out to the yard. Enid has found an old Frisbee I haven't seen in years and tosses it across the yard, encouraging Bud to fetch it. Bud doesn't move. My phone rings, and I answer, Stewart's face eventually appearing on the screen. I smile at him, and he looks . . . confused.

"Watch this," I say, switching the camera the other direction so Stewart can see the kids and Bud. I can still see his face, and he squints for a second as if trying to get his bearings. Then his eyes get wide.

"Are you kidding me? That's a *dog*?"

"He's an Irish wolfhound, and I may as well tell you now while you're thousands of miles away—he's not full-grown yet." I wait for the tirade, but it doesn't come. I watch Stewart's expression as he watches our children play with our dog. He is enthralled, shaking his head, frowning, smiling, then laughing out loud in a way I remember from years ago before our life got so complicated.

"Look at Jacob," he says, leaning into the frame so that only his forehead is visible.

"I know," I say. "Can we keep him?"

"From the looks of it, I'd say it's a done deal. Where are you? Let me see you." I switch the camera around again. "You look good, Audrey. Happy."

"Actually, I am happy," I tell him. "Things are good today. I wish you were here." I have not said that to him once since he started traveling. It's usually easier to muddle through days on my own, rather than worrying about one more person who needs a meal or attention.

"I'll be there soon enough," he says. "I hate to run, but I have the presentation in an hour."

"Good luck," I say without thinking. Usually I'm too jealous to say something like that, but right now I'm okay with what's going on here. "Let me know how it goes, and we'll see you when you get home. This is much better in person."

"Sounds good. Audrey?"

"Yeah?" I hold my breath, thinking he might say that he loves me.

"You might want to pick up another vacuum. That's a lot of fur."

My heart breaks a little, but I can't expect my entire world to change in one day. "Okay. See you soon."

I hang up and shiver as the sun dips finally out of view. I round up the kids and our dog, and we all return to the warmth that has enveloped my house today.

At bedtime, Jacob insists on dragging Bud's new bed up to his room. At first I'm hesitant, but I know that Jake won't sleep if I don't agree. I tell him Bud can sleep in his room if he leaves the door open, in case the dog needs to stretch his legs or use the bathroom during the night. I lie awake for hours, replaying the day's events and tiptoeing upstairs a couple of times to check on things. Enid has left her door open, too, and her cell phone is on the pillow next to her, but she is sound asleep. I move the phone to her nightstand and walk into Jake's room. His arm dangles over the edge of the bed, and Bud stirs at the sound of my footsteps but only raises his head in acknowledgment before quietly settling back in to his new place on the floor.

Back downstairs, I stop in the kitchen and consider pouring myself a glass of scotch or something to help me settle down and sleep. I decide against it and lie on the couch under a blanket, noticing for the first time that my house already smells different, like a dog lives here. I think about how much has happened today and how the dynamics of my family have shifted with just one decision. I know we will not be this happy every day and that our usual drama will continue, but if we can have days like this more often, maybe there is hope for us, for me.

CHAPTER SEVEN

Stewart is home from Tokyo after successfully landing the biggest project his firm has ever had. He's
in a great mood and has been working from the house
for the past few days, which has reduced my drinking
significantly, at least during daylight hours. I've felt really good, though, maybe because I've been sleeping
like a normal person, in my bed and under the covers, Stewart's quiet snoring a comfort, a reminder that
there's someone there.

Jacob's attention is still focused solely on Bud, and
Stewart observes them from a distance with quiet fascination. Enid seems happy to have her dad around, and
her disposition has improved dramatically. It's been a

nice change, and the edge is gone, even without my usual drinks.

Stewart was initially horrified to see Bud in person—apparently he appears much cuter and smaller on FaceTime—but has warmed up to him quickly. It's hard not to love the big, ugly, gentle dog whose arrival has coincided with some changes that would have been impossible to imagine just a few weeks ago.

This morning I am cooking breakfast for Stewart and me—eggs, bacon, and biscuits from scratch—when Enid floats into the kitchen and asks if she can join us. Stewart and I exchange looks of surprise, but neither of us dares to make a comment about it.

Jacob and Bud are lying in their usual spot on the living room rug, but the cooking smells prove to be too much for our lanky beast. Bud ambles into the kitchen and parks his behind on the floor next to Stewart's chair. He looks at Stewart through the long, ropy strands of fur that hang over his eyes. Sitting down side by side, he and Stewart are nearly the same height.

"Can he have bacon?" Stewart asks.

"I don't know why not," I say, "but probably not too much."

"Can I give it to him?" Enid pleads. We are all in stiff competition for the dog's heart, though none of us will ever beat Jake, who has followed Bud into the kitchen.

I nod, and Enid breaks a strip of bacon in half. She feeds a piece to Bud and puts the other in her mouth.

It's the first time I've seen her eat red meat in nearly a year. Jake wiggles his small body into his chair without pulling it out from the table. He ate his usual breakfast when he got up, but just in case, I put a biscuit on a plate in front of him now. He looks at it as if it's a foreign object and pushes it away, but he remains in the chair. Bud sits at attention for several minutes in the hopes of getting another piece of bacon before eventually lying down under the table at Jake's feet.

Right now, looking at the four of us sitting in such close proximity, I wonder if the worst is behind us. I think again of that last dinner we had at the same table and force the memory out of my mind. Maybe we can behave as a unit again. Everyone seems content. Enid is eating bacon. Jacob has been compliant about going to school and behaving there as long as Bud walks him out to the bus every morning and meets him back there every afternoon. I wonder if Jake thinks Bud spends the whole day sitting at the end of our driveway waiting for him, but it doesn't matter. Everything has been better, and I'm still pretty happy, so some wine in the evenings has been all I've needed to feel balanced. I haven't touched the vodka bottles hiding in the laundry room since Stewart has been home, and a couple of days this week, I haven't even thought about them more than once or twice when I've gotten a bit shaky. I guess when my emotions are mostly positive, I don't mind actually *feeling* them.

I wash the breakfast dishes while my family disappears to separate parts of the house, but I can still feel their presence. Our lives don't feel as separate as they used to, and I feel like we might be able to be normal again. I have secretly begun to hope that Stewart will want to spend more time at home, but when I walk into our bedroom and see that he's started laying out clothes for his next trip, I'm jerked out of the fairy tale that's begun to form in my clearer head.

I don't know why it surprises me to see his suitcase on the bed. He told me the day he got back that he would only be home a week. This is what he does. His job, regardless of why he chose it, requires him to travel all the time, and this has been our pattern for years. He packs. He leaves. He (usually) calls each day. He comes home for just long enough to have his suits dry-cleaned. Then he leaves us again. He leaves *me* again. Anger prickles at me for the first time in days, and I remind myself that he *chooses* to leave.

I start shoving socks into Stewart's dress shoes so they won't get squished in the suitcase. Stewart comes out of his closet with a stack of undershirts and boxer shorts. He is holding at least ten pairs of underwear.

"How long are you going to be gone?" I ask, pointing to the stack.

"I'm guessing probably three weeks," he says. This is news to me.

"*Three weeks?*"

"I told you that the other day, Audrey." He sounds irritated, and I know my daydream is over. "We're setting up an office in Tokyo for this project and taking some of our best people with us. I have a major role in this and need to be present. It's a huge deal for me, and the project will probably last the better part of two years. I'll be gone for a few weeks at a time because it's just too hard to fly back and forth more often than that."

I take a step back. "So you're going to be gone *more?* For a couple of years?"

"Audrey, have you listened to me at all? This is a huge . . ."

"Deal for you," I finish for him. "I heard."

He opens his nightstand drawer and throws a charger into the suitcase. "What do you want me to do about it?"

"Nothing," I snap. "I don't imagine there's much you *can* do about it. You're the big cheese, so go lead."

"What the hell is that supposed to mean?"

"I just thought you might reconsider prioritizing your family."

"Oh, come on, Audrey. I prioritize my family every time I leave. Don't you remember how hard it is to work in this business? I work eighty hours a week, and if I'm not in an office somewhere, I'm at a hotel. You, Enid, and Jacob get to live in this beautiful house without a care in the world." He rolls up a belt and shoves it into a mesh zipper pocket.

He has no idea how ridiculous and condescending he sounds. I make an exasperated noise and am about to tell him that his ego is the only thing he's prioritizing, but a bloodcurdling scream carries down the hall, and I run in the direction of the sound, not knowing what I will find.

Jacob is at the back door, beating on the glass hysterically as Bud stands nearby looking on, concerned.

"What's wrong?" I ask, leaning in, my face quickly met with a closed fist. I cover my nose with my hands as it begins to bleed profusely. This only contributes to increased hysteria from Jacob, and Bud takes two steps backward, shaking his head from side to side as if to make the noise stop.

Jacob turns away from me and yanks on the knob to the French doors, shrieking like a barn owl when they fail to open. I twist the dead bolt with bloody fingers and pull the doors open, then run to the kitchen to find Kleenex for my nose. Jacob stops screaming and goes outside. I watch through the window as Jake runs across the grass, chasing a dragonfly. He must have seen it through the back door and gotten upset when he couldn't let himself outside. That's all it takes sometimes.

Stewart wanders into the kitchen after a couple of minutes and shakes his head at the state of my face.

"Thanks for the backup," I mutter through the tissues.

"*This* is why I'm going. It's been a good week, but it won't last." He looks at the floor. "You know how people sometimes say they're '*going through a rough patch*'? Well, right now we're going through a smooth patch. The novelty of having Bud around has Jake in a really good place, and because of that, we're all in a better place."

"What's wrong with that?"

"Nothing. But when the novelty wears off, things will go back to normal—our kind of normal."

"You don't really know what our kind of normal is anymore," I say.

He sighs and leans forward, bracing himself against the island. "I can't, Audrey. I'm not equipped to handle Jake for more than a couple of days at a time. It makes me feel helpless."

"You can't, or you won't?" I start to cry, familiar with his feeling of helplessness. "You think I handle him well? Look at me!" I shout, waving a bloody tissue at my husband. "Do you honestly think we are all just '*living in this beautiful house without a care in the world*'? You have no idea how hard it is for me to do this by myself. And what about Enid? You don't want to be here for her? For any of us?"

"You don't need me because I can't help. I'm better off working, because then I actually feel like I'm *doing* something. I know you and the kids have your routine when I'm gone."

"That's ridiculous. What about this past week? I feel like we've done so well, kind of like the band has gotten back together." I smile through tears, hoping he will laugh and change his mind.

"It's temporary, Audrey. You'll see. Just let me do my job, and I'll let you do yours."

"*My* job? Stewart, the kids are *ours!*" I almost choke. "Unless you've forgotten your role in creating them."

He turns away from me and goes back to the piles of corporate clothes that cover our duvet. He hasn't even left the house yet, but I can feel that he's gone and I'm alone just like before.

By the time Stewart has left for the airport, I've had a shot of Grey Goose in the laundry room followed by two strong Cape Cods, and I'm pretty buzzed. He didn't seem to notice, but since I hadn't spoken a word to him in two hours, he had little to go on. This past week made me forget how good we are at being pissed off at each other. I wouldn't call us passive-aggressive, just apathetic.

⊷ ⊶

I manage to get Jacob and Bud settled in for the night, even though I'm not firing on all cylinders. As I pass by Enid's room, I can hear her talking, and before I can stop myself, my ear is pressed against the door, and I'm eavesdropping. She sounds chipper, happy, and something else—maybe a little bit fake? Just as I'm about to pull away and butt out of her conversation, I hear her apologize to the person on the phone.

"I really am sorry," she says. "I was mad, but what I did wasn't cool." There is a long pause before Enid speaks again.

"At least it worked out well for you," she giggles. "Maybe I did you a favor!"

I assume she's talking to Kara because otherwise I have to consider the possibility that she has someone else to apologize to. I force myself to walk away, grateful Enid has done the right thing by working through her differences with a friend. Maybe she's growing out of this difficult phase. I can only hope.

I pour myself another strong drink and lie down on the couch. I don't want to get in my bed tonight, don't even want to go into the room where my hopes were dashed earlier. I'm not sure who I'm angrier with, Stewart for leaving or myself for thinking there was a chance he wouldn't. I pull a blanket off the back of the couch and fade into the dreamless sort of sleep that will leave me feeling as if I haven't slept at all.

CHAPTER EIGHT

I wake up groggy, and Jacob is standing over me. He doesn't look happy. The clock on the mantel indicates I've overslept and already screwed up today. Jake's breakfast should be on the counter waiting by now. My head pounds as I jump up, apologizing profusely as I frantically pour Cheerios into his bowl and pull a juice and yogurt from the refrigerator.

Bud stands patiently at the back door waiting to go out for his morning pee, so I let him out and rush to get lunches packed. Jake sits at the counter, not touching his food.

"Eat, buddy," I say, realizing I haven't given him his spoon. I grab it from the drawer and set it down beside him a little too quickly, and the spoon clangs against the granite. Jake flinches and covers his ears.

"Sorry," I whisper, my second apology of the day in a matter of minutes. I fill Bud's food and water dishes and let him back inside as Enid enters the kitchen.

"Jesus, Mom," she says. "Are you sick?"

"Language, Enid. No, why?"

"You look terrible. You're wearing the same clothes as yesterday, and your hair . . ."

I try to laugh it off. "Oh, I fell asleep on the couch last night, and Jake just woke me up." I comb through my matted hair with my fingers, hoping Enid is still too young to recognize a hangover.

I shake three ibuprofen pills from a bottle and fill a glass with water while my daughter watches me from across the room. As soon as I'm alone, I'm going to have to drink something stronger to get rid of the throbbing in my temples.

"Jake," Enid snaps, turning toward her brother. "Stop feeding him Cheerios!" Jacob is holding his bowl out as Bud inhales the contents.

I grab the bowl from him and toss it in the sink. "Jacob, that's *your* breakfast. You have to eat before you go to school." I fix him a new bowl of cereal, but as soon as I put it down, he dumps it out on the floor. Bud is quicker than me and laps it up before I can get to it.

"That's the wrong bowl, Mom," Enid says as I toss the second bowl into the sink.

I want to scream as I consider the implications of a morning as disastrous as this. "Thanks for stating the obvious, Enid. I know it's the wrong bowl, but the other one is covered in dog slobber, and your brother needs to eat."

Jake climbs down from the stool, and Bud follows him down the hall. "Doesn't look like it," she says.

"Thanks for the help," I mutter, picking up Jacob's untouched juice and yogurt and putting them back in the refrigerator.

"I helped you last night," she says, so quietly I almost miss it.

"What?"

"I helped you last night. I came downstairs to look for printer paper, and you were passed out on the couch."

"I was *not*," I say, more defensively than I intend.

"Well, it sure looked that way. I shook you but you didn't move, so I poured out your drink and put the glass in the dishwasher."

I feel my face redden. "Oh. I was tired and guess I never finished it. I just sat down for a few minutes and dozed off."

She looks at me through narrowed eyes. "Why were you so tired? It was just the weekend, and Dad was home."

I turn away from her and busy myself rinsing the bowls in the sink. "Moms don't get weekends, Enid. If anything, it's busier when Dad's home because there's an extra person to take care of."

Suddenly she's standing right next to me. "Dad told me he might be gone for a month."

I frown. The time frame keeps growing without my being informed about it.

"He's got a big project at work and can't just go back and forth to Japan every week. It's too far and too expensive for the company. He'll come home whenever he can. It's a huge deal for him," I say, Stewart's ridiculous words coming from my mouth involuntarily. It's pathetic that I'm trying to convince my daughter what a superstar her dad is when I don't even believe it myself. Inside, I'm blaming Stewart for every single thing that will inevitably go wrong today.

"I'm going to change my clothes while Jake is upstairs. Eat something, okay?" I slide past her on my way out of the kitchen, picking up speed as I near my bedroom. I'm practically running by the time I reach my bathroom, where I lean over the toilet and vomit.

I wash my face and gargle with some mouthwash, considering for a brief moment swallowing the pure alcohol. I spit and throw on some jeans and a clean shirt, knowing Jake will soon be waiting by the door for his bus. My head is pounding, but I don't have time to go back to the kitchen, and Enid is already on guard. A drink is going to have to wait.

＝⊰⊱＝

When the kids are both out the door and the house is quiet, I set about regaining a level head. I wonder how the expression *the hair of the dog* came about, but it doesn't really matter as long as it works. I sit down with a drink and my cell phone, pulling up Enid's Instagram account, which I loaded onto my own phone shortly after the fake account incident and the phone call from my sister. There's no way for me to know if the girls really did delete the account, but I check her personal page more often now and even her private messages. I can't find anything that seems out of the norm for a teenage girl, but it's fascinating to see the people she chooses to follow, what she comments on, and how others respond to her posts.

She follows 514 people, and 397 follow her. That's amazing to me and more than a little frightening. I scroll through the names and photos of people she is connected with through the tiny icon on the screen and don't recognize more than a couple dozen of them. I don't think I could name three hundred people off the top of my head, and I've been on this earth three times longer than her.

Most of what I see is inane, bored kids posting pictures of themselves and their friends. A few are borderline inappropriate, but those seem to be expressly meant for generating responses. The girls make themselves appear as if they have the social lives of a Kardashian, though there aren't enough hours in the day to have as much fun as they are projecting *and* go to school and sleep. Every child's Instagram life is a carefully adjusted version of reality that edits out every single thing she is insecure about. Enid is no exception.

Enid rarely posts anything. She's had the account for almost two years and has only posted a dozen or so times. Hannah is in several of the photos, and the two of them together look young and blissfully innocent. One post I am initially surprised to see is a close-up photo of Enid and Jacob from several months ago. She must have taken it herself, but it's very artfully done—the sides of their heads are pressed together, and all you can see is their eyes, which are narrowed and squinty as though they are laughing. The caption of her post says *Happy Birthday to the sweetest little brother I could ask for!* The post has eighty-four likes, and a few of Enid's friends made comments like, *Awww!* and *Soooo sweet.*

As I look at it, I'm struck by the fact that the picture makes Jacob look like just a regular kid. His eyes alone give nothing away. It's not until you see the big picture—Jake as a *whole*—that you know he's different. Whether she realized it at the time or not, whether she intentionally left out the 90 percent of her brother that makes him stand out, she has projected a version of him that is acceptable, that nobody would ever look at twice or question. I know Enid loves her brother very much and with fierce protectiveness, but she would rather us be just a regular family, and we are anything but. I struggle with the things that make us different but can't imagine how it feels to her at this stage in her young life, when the most important thing is to be just like everyone else.

I locate Kara Abbott's page to see what sorts of things she's been putting out there. Of course there are the usual shots of multiple cute girls with their arms draped around each other, all clad in the current teenage girl uniform of skinny jeans and riding boots, soft, colorful infinity scarves enveloping each long, thin neck in a silky embrace. There are countless comments filled with tiny heart icons, friends professing their unending love for Kara and remembering *the best time ever!* Enid is not in a single post of Kara's, which doesn't surprise me, though she has commented enthusiastically on a few.

Kara has seven posts that I've found that are photos of her brother. His entire face is in every one of them. She also has a post of her mother and father standing on a beach with their arms around each other that wishes a *Happy Anniversary to the best parents ever!* I roll my eyes and shut off my phone. I can't stand having their normalcy rubbed in my face.

Bud gets up from the sunny spot near the French doors and walks on lanky legs to where I sit. He lays his chin on the table and sighs as if he's bored.

"Shall we go for a walk?" I ask. He stares at me from beneath his fringe. I grab his leash from a hook by the door and clip it on to his collar. Walking Bud is a bit like leading a horse, but it's good for both of us. He garners a similar kind of attention as Jake, curious stares and raised eyebrows, but it's much easier to let it roll off since he's a dog and not my child.

It's a beautiful day, the kind I'll be glad I ventured out into. We walk slowly down the street, every step Bud takes awkward and mechanical like a marionette. He holds his head a little higher now than he did when he first came home with us, and I believe the burden of his old life is being lifted bit by bit.

As we near the corner, I see Mrs. Speight walking our direction with Reuben. When she spots us, she slows her pace and appears to be contemplating crossing over to the other side of the street, but eventually she shortens her retractable leash and stays on our side, forcing a smile as we get closer.

"Hello, Audrey," she says, eyeing Bud warily. I squat down and give Reuben a rub on his tiny head, and Mrs. Speight inhales sharply as Bud leans down to sniff her precious baby.

"How are you today?" I have to work hard to not laugh at her horrified expression. "I promise he won't hurt Reuben," I tell her. "He's a gentle giant."

She watches closely as Bud sniffs. Reuben shakes and pees a little on the sidewalk. Done sniffing, Bud turns away, more interested in the squirrels running through the nearby yard and the cars passing on the street than the little old dog in front of him.

"Is he a service dog?" Mrs. Speight asks, still frowning, though visibly more relaxed. I think she quickly realizes that despite his size, Bud is no threat.

"A service dog?" I echo.

"For Jacob," she says, as if that explains the question.

"Jacob doesn't need a service dog. Bud is our pet, just like Reuben, only bigger." She doesn't like the comparison one bit.

"Oh, I just thought . . . with his condition. Well, never mind."

My first instinct is to be angry, but I remind myself that Mrs. Speight is old and clearly uninformed about autism.

"He's *autistic*," I say calmly. "Not blind and not suffering from a seizure disorder or posttraumatic stress. Bud has helped in a lot of ways, but he's not a trained service dog."

"He's from the pound, I remember you saying now."

"The shelter, yes."

Reuben has stopped shaking and just stands, looking up at Bud. "Well, I can't say I've been disturbed by his barking at all, so that's good at least. Enjoy your walk then, I suppose."

"Thanks. You too." I pull on the leash a little to let Bud know we're going to keep moving, and I don't look back, but I have a feeling Mrs. Speight is still watching us with her ancient, judgmental eyes.

After our stroll, I sit down and force myself to eat something, my stomach still a little sour. I catch up on emails, happy to get one updating the shelter volunteers about Frank's recovery. As I'm about to close out of email, the telltale ding alerts me to a new message. It's from Debbie Abbott, Kara's mother, inviting several girls to a sleepover for Kara's birthday next weekend. There's going to be food, music, and a "special surprise," and it all sounds lovely, except that I'm not sure why Enid has been included. The other email addresses are for parents of the girls who play a starring role on Kara's Instagram feed. Enid has never been a part of Kara's social circle and is not a girl I'd expect to be invited to something as personal as a birthday sleepover. I don't respond yet, deciding to discuss the whole thing with Enid before I RSVP. She probably won't want to go anyway, having just confessed to Kara about the Instagram situation.

The phone rings, and I look at the Caller ID. It's Stewart, probably calling to tell me he's made it to Tokyo after a grueling fourteen hours in first class. I'm too tired and hurt by him to pick it up, so I let it go to voice mail and pour myself another drink—a weak one this time, just enough to keep my headache at bay. I take the drink to my bedroom and lie on the bed, staring up at the ceiling.

Stewart and I hadn't been intimate in ages before his last visit home. With everything here so much more settled, I let my guard down and allowed myself to believe that we could get back to the way things used to be. I practically threw myself at my husband, trying desperately to feel the way I used to feel years ago.

Now I just feel stupid and pathetic, like a high school girl trying to impress the captain of the football team, while Stewart goes off on his next conquest. I roll on my side and cry with the overdue realization that my marriage is no longer a partnership, and hasn't been in a long time. Stewart has continued to live the life I wanted to live, the one I *intended* to live, before our children were born and required so much of me. I know I helped make the decision to stay home and raise them, but at some point along the way, it became less my choice and more my sentence. I can't help feeling trapped by them—Jake especially—and my career aspirations died with the onset of motherhood. Stewart keeps moving forward while I seem to stand perfectly still. His future is blazing corporate trails, but my future will look exactly like my present. I will always be here, with Enid and Jake, at least until Enid finishes school and moves out. Then it will be Jake and me, always Jake and me, because he will never be able to leave.

My eyes flutter open. I must have cried myself to sleep, and Bud is sitting by the bedside, staring at me. I wonder how long he's been there, if he heard me crying and came out of concern. But then I look at the clock and see that Jacob's bus will be here in five minutes. Bud has become a creature of habit and is ready for his buddy to come home.

I sit up, my head aching again, and give Bud a scratch. "Thanks for making sure I'm up," I say. "I can't even imagine the mess we'll have on our hands if Jake gets off the bus and we aren't there."

The ice in my drink has melted, but I gulp it down and drop the glass into the sink on my way through the kitchen. Bud follows me out the front door into the sunshine, and I sit down beside him on the warm concrete of the driveway, waiting for my future to get home from school.

CHAPTER NINE

E nid's reaction to Kara's invitation is not what I expect.

"Of *course* I want to go," she chirps. "They're the most popular girls in my grade!"

"I hate that word *popular*," I mumble.

"Well, they are, and I can't believe I got invited! Kara and I talked, and she thought it was pretty cool of me to tell her the truth about the Instagram thing, so I guess we're friends now!" She is hopping in place, her long, delicate index finger swiping dramatically on the touch pad of my laptop as she rereads Debbie Abbott's email. I don't tell her I overheard her talking on the phone to Kara.

"You *are* going to let me go, aren't you?" she asks suddenly, her hair whipping around as she turns to face me. I wish I had a reason to say no, but the only reasons I have are that I don't like what Kara said to Enid about Jake, which Enid has already handled in her own screwed-up way, and that I don't care for Kara's mother, which is petty and has nothing to do with the girls.

"Does this mean we need to go get Kara a gift?" I ask, not wanting to say yes straight out. She squeals and actually hugs me, and I can't help but bask in the unfamiliar feeling that I've made her happy. At the same time, though, it pains me that this invitation means so much to her.

"Is Hannah going?" I ask. It will be better for me and for her if one of her real friends is there.

"No," Enid says a little too quickly. "Hannah and Kara don't get along *at all*."

"Why?"

"Long story, starting in, like, fifth grade. Can we go to Kendra Scott to get Kara a present?"

"Not a chance. Will Hannah be upset that you're going to Kara's party if they don't get along?"

"I don't plan on discussing it with her," Enid says.

"She's going to know, E. It's going to be . . ." I almost say *all over Instagram,* but I catch myself. "It's going to be public knowledge if these girls are as popular as you say they are."

Enid looks at the floor. "I'm allowed to have other friends besides Hannah."

She's right. I'm not sure why I'm playing devil's advocate with her. She's been invited to what is, in her mind, the event of the year. Even though I think it will hurt Hannah's feelings, who am I to ruin it before it even happens?

"Please, can we go to Kendra Scott?" she pleads.

"Come up with a less expensive idea," I say, sitting down to type a reply to Debbie Abbott letting her know that my daughter will be in attendance at the party Saturday night.

Jacob is lying on the living room rug using Bud as a pillow while he watches *Gilligan's Island*. His eyes are bloodshot and his cheeks are flushed, so I locate a thermometer and stick it into Jake's ear, which elicits an angry screech. Bud lifts his head off the ground to see what the fuss is about.

The thermometer says his temperature is normal, but his nose is stuffy, so I give him a little cold medicine in case he's coming down with something. I open a can of chicken noodle soup for Jake's dinner and put some saltines on a plate. When the soup is warm but not hot, I call him to the kitchen to eat. He comes in wiping his nose on his sleeve and sneezes a couple of times, but he still has an appetite and seems to be in good spirits. With Bud here, Jake's spirits are almost always good now. It's made a huge difference to not be on eggshells all the time waiting for the next breakdown, though I'm afraid I've gotten complacent so that when the next one happens, it's going to throw me for a serious loop.

I realize I never checked voice mail after Stewart called earlier, so I pick up the phone and dial our code, but there are no messages. I guess he didn't feel the need to leave one when I didn't feel like answering the phone. We are definitely back to our "normal." He's happy, and I'm resentful.

I take Jacob up to run him a bath, and Bud follows as usual to sit sentry next to the tub. I pull Jake's shirt over his head and gasp at the sight of an angry red rash covering his stomach and chest. Jake scratches at his belly as he climbs into the bath. I'm going to have to take him to the doctor tomorrow, which is never pleasant. Bud scoots closer to the side of the bathtub, and Jake reaches over with a wet hand to pet him. They are such a unique pair, clinging to each other like their lives depend on it. Maybe in a way they do.

In the morning I take Jake to see Dr. Morris, the only doctor he will even remotely tolerate. Dr. Morris hands Jacob a Skittle every time he complies during the examination. It's a trick we concocted during his five-year-old checkup and have used ever since. I rarely let Jake eat candy, so each Skittle is so valuable to him that it takes his mind off what is being done and compels him to earn more. The only time Dr. Morris struggles today is getting Jake to open his mouth to inspect his throat. Jake doesn't like the little flashlight and clamps his teeth together. The doctor finally offers Jacob the rest of the bag of Skittles if he will allow him to look inside his mouth. Jake sticks out his tongue, polka-dotted with artificial coloring, and I can only imagine the hyperactivity I will have to contend with later on when an entire bag of Skittles is coursing through his bloodstream.

I'm relieved that Jacob hasn't been aggressive toward Dr. Morris during this visit, and I smile when the light is back in the doctor's coat pocket and Jacob is sorting the candy into piles on the paper that covers the examination table.

"I don't see anything that concerns me," Dr. Morris says, pumping hand sanitizer into his palm. "It could be a virus, but it looks more like an allergy to me. Did he eat anything new just before the rash showed up?"

"He hasn't eaten anything new in three years," I say. Dr. Morris chuckles, always good-humored and empathetic regarding Jacob's quirks.

"Have you changed laundry detergent? Soap? Shampoo? Household cleaners?"

I shake my head at each of these, as I am as much a creature of habit as Jacob, maybe because of him.

"Has he come into contact with any animals recently?"

"We got a dog a couple of weeks ago. The rash and sneezing just started yesterday."

The doctor rubs his hands together. "Well, he could be working up to an intolerance. Sometimes repeated exposure is what finally does it. Does Jacob touch the dog a lot?"

I think about how much of the day Jake spends using Bud as a pillow. If Jake has an allergy to Bud, it would be the cruelest irony imaginable.

"They're inseparable," I tell Dr. Morris. "Bud is like medicine to Jake." My eyes tear up, and I look away, embarrassed.

"Fortunately, it doesn't seem like a serious reaction. Certainly not life-threatening. Jacob is breathing normally, is not wheezing, and does not seem to have any airway irritation, but you need to keep an eye on him and call me immediately if he gets worse." He purses his lips, thinking. "Normally I'd suggest we look into allergy shots, but I don't think there are enough Skittles in the world for Jacob to be okay with that."

My mind runs through that scenario, and I can't imagine anything worse. "No way."

"For now let's try some over-the-counter allergy medicine, if you think he'll drink the liquid form. Watch the rash and listen for any change in breathing. There's a chance this has nothing to do with your dog, so until we know for sure, let's see how that goes."

I'm temporarily relieved but wonder if I made a huge mistake bringing Bud into our home to begin with. I agree to touch base with Dr. Morris on Monday, then take Jake's sticky, sweet-smelling hand in mine as we leave the office.

Jacob is agitated all the way home, and I'm sure it's all the sugar making him loud and defiant during our brief stop at the pharmacy. The minute we get home, however, he makes a beeline for Bud and settles down immediately. I think he just missed his best friend. How could I think for one second that Bud is a mistake? I watch Jacob nuzzle his face into Bud's neck and remember he hasn't taken the allergy medicine yet. I wrestle with him for a minute before he finally chokes the syrupy pink liquid down, and exhausted, I go to the kitchen to fix myself a drink.

When my insides are warm and tingly and I've found my equilibrium again, I tap the home screen on my phone to pull up Enid's social media page. She's at school, so I'm surprised to see recent activity on her account. She has several "likes" on a post she made just an hour ago. I'm irritated because she's not supposed to have her phone in class, but upon closer inspection, I can see that the photo was taken in the school cafeteria. I stare at the picture, trying to figure out who it's of, when realization sets in that I'm looking at my own daughter and some boy. She has on a full face of makeup and looks like she's twenty years old. It's beautiful and disgusting all at once.

The boy must be two or three years older than her, and he looks like he even has a five-o'clock shadow on his postadolescent face. His arm is draped territorially around her shoulders. Enid looks happy and scared at the same time, if that's possible. Maybe I'm imagining the scared look so that some part of my maternal brain can believe that she knows she should not be in close physical contact with this young man I don't recognize. Enid may only be feeling the happy part, for all I know.

I know she didn't look that way when she left the house this morning. Maybe the picture wasn't taken to-day—she could have posted an old one, taken before we had our talk about overdoing it—but I look again, and she's wearing the same shirt I ran an iron over this morn-ing while she ate breakfast. It cannot be a coincidence.

I press the number 37 next to the heart under Enid's post and recognize only a few of the names of people who have acknowledged her photo. Most of the likes are from boys, none of whom are familiar to me.

My eyes scan the other thumbnail photos that sit in rows on her page, but only that one has the boy in it. Maybe I'm making too much of this. Enid is in an ad-vanced math class, so he could just be an older class-mate. I explain away my worries while reading every comment from that post, cringing when I see one call-ing her *hotttttt* and stopping completely when I read a comment from *benz_a_playa* that says *Can't wait 2 hang with u Sat nite!*

Benz_a_playa? Seriously? Is it possible that Enid is involved with a boy and I'm not aware of it? And he's planning to see her Saturday night? She's supposed to be going to Kara's sleepover on Saturday. My palms start to sweat while my mind evaluates the possibilities: Enid is in way over her head and has no actual plans to see this boy on Saturday, Enid has no real plans to go to the party and *does* plan to somehow get together with this boy, or maybe *benz_a_playa* is not the boy in the photo and the comment was not meant for her.

I would like to think the last one is the right conclusion, but when I look at Enid's profile again, right underneath the quote from Eleanor Roosevelt I thought was such a mature and classy choice, is the name "Ben" sandwiched between two pink hearts. That was not there the last time I checked her page. I toss my phone onto the table like it's hot and cover my face with my hands. I have to nip this situation with my daughter in the bud before it gets out of control. She has no business being with someone like *benz_a_playa*; I don't care if he's twelve or twenty—Enid is too young to be going to school looking like she just left the Clinique counter and making plans involving boys with facial hair.

CHAPTER TEN

"You have no business stalking my Instagram page while I'm at school!" Enid shrieks when I confront her about the photo from earlier today.

"I'm pretty sure it's against school policy to be using it during school," I say, though her use of social media while at school is secondary to my concern about the boy.

"Nobody cares what we do at lunch," Enid says. "I don't even know if we have supervision during lunch." She squints like she's trying to remember ever seeing an adult in the cafeteria.

"That's not really what I'm upset about, Enid. I don't like that you appear to have a boyfriend I've never heard you mention, that you're posting photos of yourself with this boy, or that you leave the house looking your age, transform into a thirty-year-old for school, and then magically look fourteen again by the time you get home. How does that happen, and how often?"

Enid rolls her eyes.

"How do you even know him, Enid?"

"Ben's friends with Kara's boyfriend."

"Kara has a boyfriend?"

Enid looks triumphant. "Yeah, that senior, Chris, who Hannah and I told that she liked him. Apparently I should become a matchmaker or something."

Goose bumps rise up on my shoulders and arms. "Is Ben a senior?"

"Yes."

"Enid, no. There is something fundamentally wrong with this whole situation." These girls just aren't the wild, social types that a senior would find appealing without some other motive. As popular as Enid seems to think Kara is, something about this is just not right.

"What's so bad about it, Mom? He's cute and cool, and he's really sweet to me. He told me today that I'm beautiful. Why do you have to suck the happy out of everything?"

"I'm just trying to protect you. I don't want you to be taken advantage of. And what's going on with Saturday? Are you still planning to go to Kara's sleepover? Because *Ben*," I can't even say it without a hint of disdain, "seems to think he's going to see you on Saturday."

"*Yes*, Mom, I'm going to Kara's. The guys are just going to stop by for a little bit. Chris has a birthday gift for her."

"Do Kara's parents know they're coming?"

"Probably. I don't know. Don't you dare call them! What could possibly happen if they come by for a half hour? Kara's parents will be there." She glares at me, a clear warning.

"What about the other girls at the party? Will that make them uncomfortable?"

"*Real* friends are happy when good things happen to other friends." Enid picks at her fingernails like she always does when she doesn't want to make eye contact with me. I can tell she is still unsure whether any of these girls is actually her friend, but I also see her desperation to be accepted by this group.

"Just as long as you remember that you are fourteen years old and may never, under any circumstances, be alone with Ben. What's his last name, anyway?"

"*Jones*," she says, clearly irritated.

"You do understand what I'm saying, don't you?" I move so that my face is right in front of hers and she can no longer avoid looking at me. "You know what can happen to girls who don't make good decisions for themselves."

"Yes," Enid says quietly.

She stomps off to her room to do homework, and I pour myself another drink. I hate that Enid accused me of sucking the happy out of everything. I want her to be happy, but I also want her to be smart. I check on Jacob, who is lying on the carpet next to Bud, stroking his belly fur in long, slow movements. I clear my throat, and they both turn their heads to look at me. Jake's nose is still red, but I haven't heard him sneeze in a while.

"*Gilligan*'s on in ten minutes, Jake," I say, changing the channel and backtracking into the kitchen to pick up my cell phone when it starts ringing. It's Stewart, checking in before meetings begin in Tokyo. Our usual pattern has definitely resumed, though I tense up and push my resentment aside now when I answer.

I fill him in on Enid's boy situation because there is not much else to discuss, and he somewhat disinterestedly weighs the pros and cons of letting her go to the party. Stewart seems to think there is no chance that senior boys are going to be caught dead at a ninth-grade slumber party in the first place and that Kara and Enid are being led on. I think about how devastated Enid will be if that's the case, but I've warned her there's something not right about this, and honestly, I'd love to be right. Stewart convinces me to let her go, but I decide I'm going to call Kara's mom and make sure she's aware of the potential for uninvited guests. I certainly wouldn't want *my* daughter's party to be crashed by a bunch of older boys without warning.

I still don't feel great about it, but at some point, I have to let Enid navigate these situations responsibly.

I'm pretty sure she's never kissed a boy, and while I certainly had by the time I was her age, the boy I kissed was my own age and definitely not trying to take advantage of me. I've always imagined that Enid's first boyfriend would be some sweet, pimply kid from her science class, not a man-size, self-proclaimed player with a sleazy Instagram tag.

Grateful that at least I don't have to tell her she can't go to the party, I drain my glass and dial Debbie Abbott, hoping some liquid courage will make this less awkward.

When Debbie answers there is so much background noise I have to hold my phone away from my ear.

"Debbie? It's Audrey Anderson. Am I catching you at a bad time?" It sounds as if she is standing in the middle of a party, loud voices and music drowning out her greeting.

"Oh, hi, Audrey. Give me a second—I'm just going to run outside where I can hear you better." The sounds muffle a bit, and I wait for her to speak again. "Audrey? Are you there?"

"Yes, did I catch you in the middle of something?"

"Oh no, no," she says. "Kara has some school friends here, and they're a noisy bunch!"

I imagine how Jacob would react if Enid's friends came here and made that kind of racket. I don't think *I'd* handle it well, either, but Jake would be under his bed in the fetal position with his hands over his ears. I wonder if it bothers Thomas at all.

"Do you have a minute to talk?" I ask.

"Sure! What's up?"

I clear my throat, feeling like a tattletale. "Well, Enid is very excited about Kara's party on Saturday. It was so nice of you to include her."

"The girls will have a great time. Don't tell Enid, but I've got some ladies from the day spa coming to give them manicures, pedicures, and facials!"

I inspect the fingernails on my left hand and can only imagine. Enid will be over the moon. "Wow," is all I can say.

"I know! I can't believe my baby girl is turning fifteen. She's all grown-up!" Debbie's voice overflows with enthusiasm, but all I can think is that fifteen isn't even close to grown-up.

I'm silent for a moment, hoping for an obvious time to bring up the subject I called about, but decide to just launch into it. "Well, speaking of *all grown-up*, I'm calling because of something Enid mentioned to me earlier." I pick up my glass to take a fortifying sip, forgetting that it's empty. Disappointment washes over me.

"This is awkward, but apparently Enid and Kara have . . . for lack of a better word . .. boyfriends," I continue. "Boyfriends who are seniors, and who plan to stop by your house during the party on Saturday night."

There is a long pause before Debbie responds. "Excuse me? I think you must be confusing Kara with someone else. Kara doesn't have a boyfriend."

"Are you sure? Enid told me that Kara's boyfriend, Chris, introduced Enid to his friend, Ben. I saw a picture of Enid and Ben on Instagram." I sound like an idiot.

"Have you seen pictures of Kara and a boy *on Instagram*?"

I stop and think. Kara's posts are all of her girlfriends and her family. My daughter is the one posing with a boy for the world to see.

"Well, no, but Enid said . . ."

"Maybe Enid has a boyfriend who's a senior and wants you to think she's not the only one dating outside her appropriate age group." Debbie's accusing voice has lost any trace of sweetness.

"I don't know why she would do that," I say. It hadn't occurred to me that Enid could be lying about this, but I suppose anything's possible. "I guess I need to have another talk with Enid."

"I guess so," Debbie says, sweet again. "Kids this age say a lot of things to stay out of trouble, but I can assure you my daughter does not have a boyfriend who is a senior. I just wouldn't hear of such a thing."

I apologize and hang up, embarrassment heating my cheeks. My attempt to inform another mother has resulted in my own parenting being called into question by Debbie Abbott. Why can't I seem to do anything right when it comes to Enid? She warned me not to call, and now I feel like a fool. Light-headed, I decide against

Kimberly Conn

another cocktail and figure out what's for dinner. Bud comes into the room alone when I dump a scoop of dog food into his bowl. I look around the corner into the living room and find Jake curled up on the floor, sound asleep. The doctor visit must have worn him out.

I find a box of spaghetti and a jar of sauce, one of the few things Jacob and Enid will both eat, and put a pot of salted water on the stove to boil. Then I take a deep breath and go upstairs to talk to my daughter, frankly a bit terrified of how it's going to go.

Enid is stoic, though her eyes convey surprise when I tell her about my conversation with Debbie Abbott.

"I told you not to call her," she says calmly.

"I didn't feel I had a choice. Dad and I decided that your well-being is more important."

"You told Dad?"

I should reach out and touch her to show her I'm not the enemy she seems to think I am, but I can't when she's looking at me with such disgust. I stand at a distance with my arms crossed. "Of course. You're his daughter, too."

"Since when do you care what Dad thinks?" Her face becomes expressionless again, and I reject the impulse to defend Stewart and make him out to be a martyr who has no choice but to travel all the time, working hard for the sake of his family. *We* are the martyrs—Enid, Jacob, and me—living day to day without backup.

"You're dodging the issue, Enid. Mrs. Abbott said there's no chance Kara is in any kind of relationship with a senior. This is uncharted territory for you. Is that why you said what you did about Kara? So I'd think you weren't the only one?"

"I'm *not* the only one. If Kara's mom thinks I made Chris up to keep myself out of trouble, it's only because Kara doesn't want her mom to know about him. Trust me, Chris is a real person and had his *real* hand on Kara's *real* butt after school today." She sits down heavily on her bed and kicks off her flats. "Thank God Mrs. Abbott didn't believe you, at least," she says.

"You say that like it's a good thing. I felt like an idiot when she questioned my intentions." I look at her tiny feet and remember her as a little girl. A maternal wave I don't often feel anymore where Enid is concerned flutters for a moment in my heart. I wish I felt more like a caregiver and protector than judge and jury.

"It is, because if Mrs. Abbott believed you and confronts Kara about it, then I'm out. For good."

"Out? Like this is some kind of club? Well, if the boys show up at the Abbotts' house Saturday night, she's going to know I was right. Then what?"

"You better hope that doesn't happen." Again, no emotion, but it's definitely a warning. She stands up again and kicks her shoes to the side before walking over to her desk, turning her back on me. "I've got lots of homework left to do."

I almost leave without saying anything else, but as my hand wraps around the doorknob, I stop. "Enid, if Kara stops being your friend because of that, she wasn't your friend to begin with."

She sighs, flipping open a textbook. "That's easy for you to say. Is that why you don't have any friends, Mom?"

It's amazing how easily she can identify and attack my weak spots, but I can't argue her point, so I ignore it. "Do you think going to the sleepover is the right thing?" I ask.

"It's everything," she says without looking at me. She plops down in her desk chair. I stand for at least a minute, but when she doesn't turn around again, even in annoyance that I haven't left yet, I close her door silently and leave.

I wish friendships could be easier for Enid than they have been for me. I often blame Jacob for driving a wedge between me and the people who find it hard to be around us—Jake can be difficult to wrap one's brain around, and I'm usually so wound up that I'm not the least bit fun or interesting to be around— but I also know that I'm at fault, too, because I have built a protective wall around Jacob, and when I laid the last brick, I was inside the wall with him. Enid shouldn't have to work so hard for the approval and inclusion of these girls. They should *want* to be her friend because she's smart, adorable, and, with just about everyone but me, kindhearted. She'd make a great friend if she just didn't have to spend so much time strategizing.

Heading back to the kitchen, I drop pasta into the water now bubbling on the stove and check in on Jake. He's still asleep on the floor, and Bud is right next to him, their heads touching. *Their* friendship is unconditional. Bud doesn't care that Jacob throws fits or can't express himself very well, and it has never occurred to Jake that Bud's gangly appearance or sad past make him unfit to love. I wish Bud could live forever so that Jake will always have a friend.

As I stand over them, Jake stirs, and his eyes flutter open. He looks at me and smiles, and I realize that Jake is my one true friend, too. He needs me regardless of how impatient I am, how embarrassed I get because of his outbursts, and how much I've had to drink. I think needing me is his way of loving me, and since I'm so alone, by choice or not, I need Jake, too.

Enid takes her dinner up to her room, saying she's behind on an English paper. I think she wants to avoid being in a room with me, forcing conversation or enduring equally painful silence. Honestly, I'm relieved not to have to do either.

I cut Jake's spaghetti noodles into tiny pieces so he can scoop them up with his spoon. Long noodles frustrate him, but for some reason, he won't eat any other pasta shape. By the time he's done eating, he has sauce all over his cheeks and lips, and when he gets up to go take his bath, Bud helps speed the process by licking the Bolognese from his face. Jake grunts and swats him away, annoyed for the first time by Bud's offering of affection, but then takes the dog by the collar and gently leads him up the stairs like he does every night.

I dump his dinner plate in the sink and follow my best friend and his best friend up for bath time.

CHAPTER ELEVEN

Enid stays calm and unusually in control of her emotions for a couple of days. When we go shopping for a birthday gift for Kara, I let Enid pick out a new pair of cute pajamas for the party, which are now neatly packed inside her overnight bag. I have heard nothing more about Ben—most likely because Enid wants me out of her business—and she's gone silent on Instagram, making no new posts or comments that I've been able to find.

We stop by the animal shelter on the way to Kara's house because I want to say hello to Frank, who's just returned to work part-time after his heart attack. Enid stays in the car so that she doesn't "smell like an abandoned dog" when she arrives at the party. I want to remind her that Bud was once an abandoned dog, but I bite my tongue and lead Jake through the door, with Bud close behind on his leash. Frank grins from ear to ear when he sees us and gives Bud an energetic scratch behind the ears. Bud shakes nervously, and I wonder if he remembers being left here, but Jacob stands at his side with his hand wrapped around a clump of fur, as if to assure his friend that he's not going anywhere without him.

"He looks like a different dog, Audrey," Frank says, giving Jake a small wave. "Hi, Jacob! Are you taking good care of Budweiser?" He looks at me. "Do you still call him that?"

"He's just Bud now," I say.

"That suits him." Frank smiles. "I'm so glad everything worked out for him."

"It's been great for all of us," I assure him.

We talk for a few minutes about Frank's recovery, and while he looks thin, his voice is strong, and his enthusiasm hasn't waned a bit. It's a relief to know he's back here taking care of things like usual.

"I'm not coming in to volunteer as much anymore," I tell him. "I feel bad leaving Bud alone while the kids are at school."

He winks at me. "Then I've done my job. Every animal that leaves here with a good family is a win in my book, and I'm not sure many people would have found room in their hearts—or homes—for Bud. It looks to me like he's got all the love he can handle." Jake is murmuring into Bud's ear, sending his tail into a slow wag.

We say goodbye and head back to the car, where Enid sits, giggling into her phone. It's the most cheerful I've seen her in several days. She hangs up as soon as I open the back door to let Bud climb in, and by the time I get behind the wheel, she's straight-faced again. I don't ask whom she was talking to, since I'm not sure I'd get an honest answer. I can't wait for this stupid party to be over so we can just move on.

When I pull into the Abbotts' driveway, Enid jumps out of the car with her bag and hurries toward the front door before I can even shut off my engine. I roll the back windows down and leave Jacob and Bud in the car, following my daughter up the walkway. The door is ajar and Enid is already inside, so I call out into the foyer, uncomfortable just walking into the house.

Teenage squeals are coming from the kitchen, and I can pick out my daughter's voice gushing over the birthday girl. "Oh my gosh, Kara, your house is *so* pretty," and "You got tickets to Taylor Swift for your birthday? Your parents are the coolest." I sigh and wait patiently to be greeted. Debbie comes hurrying around the corner, licking pink frosting from a spatula.

"Audrey! Come in." She beckons me with the spatula.

"I can't; I left Jacob in the car with the dog. I just wanted to say hello and thank you for having Enid." I hesitate for a second and add, "I'm really sorry about my phone call the other day. I hope I didn't upset you."

She waves the spatula dismissively. "Don't be silly. These girls . . ."

I don't know what she means by that—if she still thinks Enid lied and is chalking it up to simply being an adolescent female, or if she knows there was some truth to it and doesn't want to admit it. "Well, it was rude of me to bombard you with all that," I say.

"You were just trying to be helpful."

I bristle, feeling like a complete idiot apologizing for trying to do the right thing. I am about to say thanks and goodbye and just leave when Debbie's eyes look past me and spot Bud's giant head sticking out of the back window of my car.

"Dear Lord," she says, walking toward him. "Is that your *dog*?"

I laugh, remembering Enid's reaction the day we brought him home. "Don't let his looks deceive you. He's as sweet and gentle as he is big."

Debbie reaches out and pats Bud awkwardly on top of his head. Jake peers around Bud's massive body to see who's touching his dog.

"Hi, Jakey, remember me?" Debbie says in a high-pitched voice, flashing a wide, manic smile at my son. I forgot she used to call him that, back when Jacob and Thomas were in the same preschool class.

"*Jake,*" I say, "can you say hello to Mrs. Abbott?" Of course I know he won't, and instead he leans back into his booster seat, hiding behind Bud. I don't blame him.

"He's gotten so big," Debbie says. *Of course he's grown,* I think. *You haven't laid eyes on him in close to three years.* "How is he doing at that school?"

That school? I clench my teeth, wishing I could just get in the car and drive away. "Great, thank you. They're so good with the kids there. How is Thomas doing at *his* school?" *See, you moron? Our kids are* different.

Her face lights up, an invitation to tell me stuff I'm not interested in hearing. She rattles on for several minutes about his academic prowess and the technology club he joined, *the youngest student ever to be allowed to join!* I'm grateful when Bud lets out a bark, giving me an excuse to leave the conversation.

"I'd better get going," I say politely. "Thanks again."

"So nice to see you, Audrey. I've got to go get the Chinese food ordered before the spa shows up!" She turns and hurries back into her house, where she will spend the entire evening delighting my daughter and spoiling her princess. It makes me sick.

As I climb into the driver's seat, Bud barks again, and this time I understand what he is communicating. I get out and open the back door, letting him unfold his long legs and climb out. He takes a few steps into the Abbotts' side yard, takes a wolfhound-size poop, and pees on the mailbox post before rejoining Jake in the car. I tell him he's the best dog in the world and drive home.

━╪╾ ╾╪━

Jacob is in bed after a minute-long sneezing fit and a dose of allergy medicine that makes him sleepy. I am beginning to wonder if he might really be allergic to Bud, but my brain pushes away thoughts of the obvious solution.

I'm on my fourth drink, my nerves about Enid just a vague annoyance now. If boys show up at the party, it's not my problem. Maybe Debbie Abbott won't act so smug next time if I end up being right.

I stretch out on the couch with my drink and my phone. Certain the girls are documenting every second of their pampering for the uninvited world to see (poor Hannah), I scroll through Instagram expecting to see a photo of Enid looking cozy with her new group of friends. To my surprise, there is nothing. I even search Kara's page, but no new posts have been made there since yesterday.

Relieved, I send Enid an olive branch via text message. *Hope you're having fun. Good night!*

I wait for the little bubbles that indicate she's texting me back, but I stare at the screen until my eyes cross. I toss my phone onto the side table and decide to have a nightcap before I head to bed.

＝◄┼ ┼►＝

When my phone rings, I'm disoriented. I must have dozed off . . . or passed out. I'm still on the couch, and all the lights are on. I reach for the phone, Enid's name lighting up on the screen.

"Enid?" I sit up, the room spinning.

"Mom?" She sounds like she's crying. "Can you come get me?"

"What time is it?" My eyes can't focus on the clock across the room.

"I don't know. Late." She sniffles. "You have to come get me."

"What's the matter? Are you sick?"

Enid stammers into the phone incoherently, something about a text message and Ben.

"Slow down. I can't understand you," I say.

Her words are garbled and punctuated with gasps for breath. "Took a picture of me . . . Ben forwarded it to people . . . Mrs. Abbott took our phones . . . Everyone has seen me naked!"

"What?" I jump up, my heart racing. "Ben has a naked picture of you? How in God's name did that happen?" I'm suddenly furious with myself for letting her go to the party and even more furious for hoping something like this would happen, just not to my daughter.

"You took a picture of yourself naked and sent it to a boy? Enid, how can you be so stupid?" I'm yelling, saliva flying from my mouth as my stomach churns.

"Mom, *I* didn't take it. Or send it!" I've heard her upset but never like this. "Kara's mom collected all our phones because she said she wanted us to actually *talk* to each other tonight. My phone was in a basket in the kitchen until an hour ago. When she gave it back to me, there was a text from Ben telling me I'm a flat-chested loser . . ." She breaks off, and I hold my breath for her to finish. "So I scrolled back, and a picture of me getting undressed was sent to him. From *my* phone, which I didn't even *have!*"

"Give me Ben's number. I'm going to call him right now and demand . . ."

"Mom, it's too late. He forwarded it to some of his friends, and they forwarded it to even more. Hannah just called me to tell me her sister got it from some guy in her AP History class." She breaks down completely, and I'm frozen. "Mom?"

A million thoughts go through my mind, not one of them clear. "Okay, let me think. I've got to get Jake out of bed—I can't leave him here alone. I'll be there as soon as I can. Where are Mr. and Mrs. Abbott? Do they know?"

"Mrs. Abbott is in the kitchen talking to the other girls. I'm hiding in the bathroom. Someone snuck my phone out of the basket and took that picture, Mom, but nobody will admit it! Please come get me, Mom. What am I going to do?" She begins to sob again, and I feel like I'm going to faint; everything is moving too fast.

"Get your things and wait by the door. I'm coming."

"Okay."

"Enid?"

"Yeah?"

"Everything is going to be okay." But even as I say it, I don't know if it's true. I've imagined situations where Enid has to decide about kissing boys, even having sex with them, but never this. I'm completely unprepared for this.

I hang up and call Stewart's cell phone, not the least bit concerned with what time it is in Tokyo or what important thing he might be doing right now, but I'm greeted by his horribly businesslike voice mail. I leave a scattered, hysterical message as I run upstairs to yank my sleeping son out of his bed. He fusses and squirms in my arms, and by the time I get him buckled into the car, he is crying and banging his head violently against the headrest.

"Jacob!" I yell at him, flustered. "Stop it!" This has the opposite effect from the one I intend, sending his screams into a volume and pitch I've never heard before. I don't know how I'm going to get to Enid with this going on in the back seat. I slam the door to muffle the sounds and press my fingers to my temples to ease the throbbing. I wonder if I should have just left him in bed—he might never have known I was gone. But it's too late now, and if he woke up for some reason and I wasn't there, there's no telling what he might do. He could leave the house looking for me or launch himself into a fit of panic that I cannot even begin to imagine the repercussions of. Leaving Jake at home is not an option *ever*, reminding me of what I have in store for me for the rest of my life. Where I go, Jacob goes.

Jake's hollering continues from inside the car, and I notice that there is another god-awful noise coming from the house. I open the door to find Bud standing on the other side, howling. Exasperated, I pull him out the door and shove him into the car, too. Thank goodness this immediately quiets Jacob, whose face is now blotchy, swollen, and streaked with tears. Maybe where I go, Jake *and* Bud go.

Finally able to pull out of my garage, I skid out of my driveway on damp pavement, the fleeting awareness that I should not be behind the wheel quickly shoved aside by concern for Enid and a deep, seething anger. It has been raining for the past few hours, and a light fog rises up from the warm asphalt. I clutch my cell phone with one hand, ready to answer if Enid or Stewart calls, and the steering wheel with the other.

My mind races, trying to make plans for what I'm going to do and say when I get to the Abbotts' house. I envision myself stomping into the kitchen, where Debbie is holding court with the other girls and demanding an explanation and admission of guilt. I will take my daughter by the hand and lead her away from these fake friends, telling her that I, for once, will be the one she can rely on.

Jacob is still sniffling in the back seat, but when I glance over my shoulder, I see the shadowy figure of Bud, whose head is resting on Jake's lap in a show of solidarity against the crazy woman who has disrupted their night. Forcing myself to focus on the road, I press down on the accelerator. The roads are empty at this hour, so my car blows through the accumulating puddles at twice the speed limit. I may have let myself drink more than usual tonight, but right now I feel totally in control.

The drive seems endless, but I finally turn into the Abbotts' subdivision.

"*Maaa*," Jacob pleads from his booster.

"I know, buddy," I say. "I'm sorry. We're going to get Enid, okay? Almost there."

"*Maaa*," Jake says again. Bud whines.

The smell hits me at the exact moment I hear the noise, and I realize that Jacob has thrown up all over the back seat. I've been driving like a maniac and made him carsick. My mistakes are piling up. I wonder again if I should have just left him in bed, but that could have proved to be my biggest mistake of all. No, my biggest mistake was letting Enid go to that godforsaken party to begin with.

I reach back to pat Jacob on the knee, apologies and sympathy pouring from my mouth. The dog has inched away from Jake and is sitting up now, clearly concerned. My cell phone rings, startling me, but I know it's either Enid wondering why we're not there yet or Stewart returning my call. Turning the phone over in my hand to answer it, I completely miss the stop sign and don't see the van crossing the intersection until I am hurtling through it at fifty miles an hour. When I hit the van, my phone is next to my ear, but I haven't said hello yet.

CHAPTER TWELVE

The lights and sounds are unfamiliar—reds and blues and lots of voices. A man speaks to me in a loud voice, and for a moment I think it might be Stewart. He called me, but I don't remember talking to him. My head is killing me, and I remember the drinks I had at home, too many of them. It smells like puke and something pungent and chemical.

My brain begins to sort through more memories. Jacob threw up. Where is Jacob? He's in the back seat of my car. I remember now.

"Ma'am?" the man asks again. It's definitely not Stewart.

"Jacob!" I call, turning in my seat toward where he was sitting. White fabric blocks my way, and I swat at it, pain screaming through my entire body.

"Ma'am, please, we need you to stay calm. You've been in an accident. What's your name?"

"Where is Jacob?" I lean back as the man reaches into the car and pushes the white stuff away from me. It's the airbag, and I start to panic. Broken glass speckles the dashboard. I turn again to see that the back doors of my car are open and the back seat is empty, Jake's booster lying on its side, smeared with something red. What have I done? "What happened to Jacob?"

The man asks my name again, and I give it to him. "Where is Jacob?"

"Is Jacob your son? We got him out, and he's being put in an ambulance." He shines a flashlight on me. "Audrey, can you tell me what hurts?"

I don't know what to tell him. Everything hurts, but all I care about is Jacob. "I'm fine. I need to see Jacob." I make a move to get out of the car, but the seat belt is holding me in.

"Ma'am—Audrey—you need to be still. Jacob is in the ambulance being treated. Is there someone we can call? A family member?" I look at the man for the first time. He's in firefighter's clothes.

"My husband is in Japan. I tried to call him. I need to see Jacob!"

"Audrey, you can't see Jacob right now. We need to get you out of the car and assess your injuries. You've been in a bad accident." He is calm and direct, like a robot, which is irritating.

"I need to see Jake." I squirm, not caring how badly it hurts.

"You can't see him right now, but if you will be still, this will go faster, and we can get you to him." Another fireman walks up with a long board that he lays on the ground beside the car.

"I need to see him. You have to let me see my son!" Yelling hurts, too, but I need to see Jake more than I need to talk to the fireman.

He crouches down so he can look me in the eye. "Jacob is hurt pretty bad. He needs immediate treatment, and it looks like you do, too. Now, is there anyone we can call to meet Jacob at Children's Hospital? You'll be going to Elmwood Medical Center."

It all hits me at once. I was on my way to get Enid. I never got there. She is still with those horrible girls. "My daughter is just down the street. I was coming to get her." I stop to breathe between racking sobs. "I was almost there. She was very upset."

"Okay, Audrey. Let's get you out of the car, and we'll call your daughter so she doesn't worry." The firemen slide me from my seat and gently rest me on the backboard. One of them wraps a towel or something around my head and then secures straps around me. They lift me up, and the movement takes my breath away, pain shooting through my legs and back.

All I can think of is my children until I'm carried past the van I hit. It's crushed in the middle on one side. My God, I did that.

"I didn't see it until I was—" It's getting harder to breathe. "Did I . . . was anyone else hurt?"

"Audrey, you need to calm down. Let's worry about you for a minute."

Worry about me? Look at what I've done. Jacob is in an ambulance, and they won't let me see him. I crashed into another vehicle, and the fireman won't tell me if anyone was injured. I'm sure they aren't telling me because I can't handle the answers. What if Jacob dies? What if the people in the van die? I'm suddenly more hysterical than I've ever been in my entire life.

I'm placed in the back of an ambulance where the overhead lights are blinding as I writhe to get loose of the restraints. A new person, a woman, urges me to calm down, but I think I've lost my mind. I scream at her and demand to see Jacob. The first fireman is crouching by my feet, watching me cautiously, as if I'm a rabid animal.

"Ma'am," he says, "if you calm down and let them take a look at you, I'll go see what I can find out about your son." The female paramedic sticks a needle in my arm, and a burning sensation follows the prick.

I stop fighting and nod, tears turning him into a shapeless blob. "He's autistic," I tell him, for once not embarrassed to say it out loud. "He doesn't really talk."

"That's good to know. I'll go tell the paramedics. Anything else?" He touches my shoe with a kind hand.

"His dog, the one that was in the car with us. He's Jacob's best friend and will help calm him down if he's scared."

"I'm sorry," he says, patting my foot one more time. "The dog didn't make it." He grimaces as he climbs out of the ambulance, grateful, I'm sure, to have a reason not to watch my next breakdown.

When the fireman comes back to tell me that Jacob's ambulance has already left to take him to Children's Hospital, my tears are silent, and I'm exhausted from my hysteria. The fireman already told me I'm going to a different hospital. My son needs me more right now than he ever has in his life, and I cannot be there for him. The fact that I am the reason for this makes me numb all over, and I wish that *I* could die, to take the place of the others or so I don't have to live another second with the guilt of what I've done.

Just as they are about to close the doors of the ambulance, I hear the one thing that gives me hope: Enid's shouts from outside. She is demanding to see me and forces her way into the ambulance with Debbie Abbott on her heels, breathless and in pajamas.

"Mom, what happened?"

The paramedic graciously explains the situation so I don't have to. Debbie covers her nose and mouth with her hands and stares at me wide-eyed. I reach up to hold Enid's hand, and she holds on until she learns that her brother has been seriously injured and is on his way to the hospital. My hand falls back to my side with a thud. I wince.

"He can't be there alone," she tells everyone in ear-shot. "He will come unglued." She's right. If he is in a huge, bustling building full of strangers and noises he's never heard, constant beeps and paging, he will shut down or freak out. That's if, God willing, he's even conscious.

"Someone needs to take me to where my brother is!" she hollers, taking control, looking around for a volunteer.

Debbie is shaken from her trance and speaks up for the first time. "I'll take you, honey. I'll stay with you and Jacob as long as you need me to." I'm not sure if this last part is directed at me or at Enid, but I'm grateful. She's not the person I'd choose to help my children through something like this, but it's my fault we're here, and at least she kind of knows what she's dealing with . . . with my kids, at any rate.

"Enid, what about . . ." I'm afraid to say it in front of Debbie, afraid to upset Enid further, but I don't want to leave anything hanging. "What about the text?"

Debbie picks up the hand that Enid let go of and gives it a gentle squeeze. "Audrey, don't worry about that. Bob is handling it. I know it's important to get that situation taken care of, but *this* situation is more time sensitive. You need to let them take you, and I'll take Enid to be with Jacob." She squeezes again and gives me a look of such pity, I start to cry again. I never thought Debbie Abbott would be my savior.

"Enid, call Dad on the way. He called me right before . . ."

"I'll call him, Mom. I'm going to go now."

"Take care of Jake."

"I promise." She turns to the paramedic. "Take care of my mom."

My daughter is being forced to become an adult right in front of my eyes, and I don't know which of the challenges she's been confronted with tonight will prove greater for her to overcome.

Enid and Debbie leave the ambulance, and a paramedic I haven't seen yet climbs in. He has paperwork for me to sign, giving consent for the medical treatment Jacob will need in my absence. I'm now an absent mother. Jake has two absent parents. What did he ever do to deserve this?

"Have you seen my son?" I ask him.

"Yes, he's headed to Children's. It's possible he will need surgery—he sustained some internal injuries during the crash. The dog took the most impact, though, because he was unrestrained. We'll know more about your son once we get him to the ER." He takes the paper from me and disappears, now replaced by a police officer.

The policeman's eyes have bags underneath them, and his attitude matches his apparent lack of sleep.

He seems jaded compared to the firemen, and when he starts asking me questions about the accident and the moments leading up to it, I can tell by the way he looms over me that he's not going to leave until I talk. I tell him about Jake getting carsick and about trying to soothe him. I tell him about my cell phone ringing, and that was why I took my eyes off the road. I even tell him about the reason I was hurrying to that part of town in the middle of the night with my son and dog in the car. Poor Bud. Remembering all of it hurts so much I start crying again, so hard that I hyperventilate, and the medic covers my face with an oxygen mask. She shoos the officer away, telling him he can talk to me at the hospital after I've been treated.

I don't tell the officer about the drinks.

CHAPTER THIRTEEN

The ambulance ride is eternal, and I lie still and quiet while the paramedic shines lights into my eyes and palpates my body from top to bottom. I don't care what's wrong with me. I would still rather die on the way to the hospital than face what I've done to my son, our dog, and the people in the van. I have gotten no more updates on Jacob and have no idea what they've done with Bud.

I lie on a stretcher in the emergency room triage hallway for a long time before being moved to a room. The same cranky police officer from the crash scene came to finish his interrogation but was kind enough to bring my purse and phone, which were retrieved from my car before it was loaded onto a wrecker. My phone screen is cracked, but it works, though service inside the hospital is terrible. At least I'm saved from having to talk to Stewart just yet, because I am totally not ready for that.

I keep reminding myself it was an accident, but I know it could have been prevented if I had made different choices. I don't know if all the facts will come out, but I'm terrified of what will happen to me if they do.

I tell my nurse I'm sick to my stomach, and she helps me to the bathroom. "It's going to hurt if you throw up, Audrey; I'm just warning you. Broken ribs don't mess around."

In addition to two broken ribs, I have a separated shoulder. Everything else is superficial. I close the bathroom door and lean against the wall, glad for the relative quiet. Out of the corner of my eye, I see my reflection in the mirror and turn toward it. My face looks like it's been through a bar brawl. Ironic, I think, since I haven't set foot inside an actual bar in years. I do all my drinking in private. My eyes are the only part of me I'd recognize, but only because of the familiar sadness set so deep within them.

For the first time, I wonder what in the world I've had the right to be so unhappy about before tonight. It's selfish to be resentful of Jacob because he makes my life more complicated, and unbelievably shallow to think I'm the only mother who feels alienated from my teenage daughter. I've never stopped to consider that perhaps Enid's sullenness and disdain are exactly what I've modeled for her. There have been a hundred times I've thought of saying no to her about something but haven't because I'd simply rather not deal with the fallout. At what point did I surrender the responsibility of being her mother?

The phone rings in my hospital room, and I move too quickly to answer it in case it's Enid or Debbie. I have to stop and catch my breath, my injured shoulder and ribs protesting every movement. The nurse waits patiently outside of the bathroom door as I emerge, panting.

"They'll call back," she assures me, but it's not reassuring at all. She helps me ease my sore body into the bed, and as she leaves the room, the policeman from earlier holds the door open for her. He says something to her that I cannot hear before knocking on the doorjamb and walking in before I can invite him. I notice his nameplate for the first time—*Brewer*. How appropriate.

Braced for more questions and reliving the horrible events again, I'm relieved when Officer Brewer tells me he has some good news.

"The driver of the van has been released with just a few scrapes." It is good news, but not the news I was hoping for.

"There was only one person in the van?"

He nods. "A plumber who was finishing up at an emergency call. You hit him dead center on the passenger side, but there wasn't much on board other than . . . well, you know . . . plumbing stuff."

I exhale, my heart rate slowing a bit. I'm grateful nobody else has been hurt too badly by this, just my own family.

"Is there anything else you can remember about the events leading up to the accident, Mrs. Anderson? Do you know what speed you were going?" He seems less intimidating to me now, but I still don't like him being here.

I raise my eyes to meet his without moving my head, more from shame than from a sore neck. "No, I can't remember anything else, and I honestly don't know how fast I was driving. Like I told you, I was hurrying to get my daughter, who was very upset. Jacob started throwing up, and I reached back to comfort him, and then my phone rang. I was waiting for my husband to return my call about the—stuff with my daughter. I was distracted by all of it, and when I tried to answer my phone, I missed the stop sign. I'm so, so sorry." I start crying again.

"Okay," he says, but he stands and just looks at me, clearly in no hurry to leave. "Where is your husband? Is he with your son?"

I shake my head. "He's not here. He's working in Japan. My daughter is with Jacob because I'm here. I know the accident was one hundred percent my fault, but it was an *accident*. I appreciate you coming to tell me about the other driver." Tears pour from the corners of my eyes again, and I know it's going to be a very long time before I go a day—or an hour, even—without crying. "I was worried that since it was a van . . ."

"There were more people inside?" Officer Brewer finishes for me. I nod, and a sad, pathetic noise escapes my mouth.

"And now that I know I haven't killed a van full of people, I'd just like to know that I haven't killed my own son, either." My body shakes, and it hurts. I deserve to feel miserable and will gladly endure a lifetime of this pain if it means Jacob will be okay. I will get him another dog if that's what he wants, though I wonder if Bud can ever be replaced. I will never again feel sorry for myself that I have an autistic child. I will do a better job with both of my children, I will look for the best in them, and I will tell Stewart that I can't do it alone. I need human support more than I need alcohol to fill the void.

The nurse comes back in carrying a tray, which she sets down on the bed next to me. I recognize the items on the tray immediately and know she is here to draw blood. Panic surges through me, and I have the immediate thought to kick the tray off the bed and run from the room. I had my last drink hours ago, but I know any blood test I take now will show that I still have alcohol in my system. Officer Brewer is watching my reaction carefully, and I feel certain he knows exactly what I'm thinking.

"I need you to consent to a blood alcohol test," he says uncomfortably while the nurse pulls on latex gloves. He does not look directly at me now. "It's standard protocol. We have no reason to suspect that alcohol was a factor in your accident"—his eyes flicker in my direction for a split second—"but if you don't consent, we can issue a warrant."

I feel cornered, though I know I've put myself in this situation. If I decline, it's an admission of guilt. If I consent, the test will be my admission of guilt, but at least I don't have to be judged in this room right now.

The nurse tears open a foil package containing an alcohol swab. She holds it between two fingers and looks at me. "Okay?"

"Yes," I tell her. She hands me a ball to squeeze, and I close my eyes, imagining what my life will be like once I am arrested. Tears manage to make their way between my tightly shut eyelids, and when the nurse is done, I open my eyes again, and she pats my knee.

"I'm sorry if that hurt," she says, though the prick of the needle never even registered.

Officer Brewer looks pale and, for once, sympathetic. "Thanks, Tina," he says to her. I wonder how he knows her name. Maybe they meet under these circumstances often. I'm just another drunk who's caused problems that they have to handle. Tina slips the vials of my blood into a special padded envelope, signs a piece of paper, and watches as Brewer signs his name as well. They are making my unraveling official.

I lie back and roll away from them, unable to stop the flood of regret that pours from me. I deserve whatever punishment I receive, but still not knowing how Jacob is may be what kills me. I hear the door to my room open and close, so when Officer Brewer clears his throat to let me know he is still here, it startles me.

"What can I do to help you?" he asks. The tone of his voice has changed, softened.

"I just want to be able to take care of my kids," I say after I'm able to catch my breath. "Just let me do that. They're alone without me, and I know *I did this*, but they need me."

I feel a heavy hand on my shoulder, but I still don't turn over. "Give me your boy's full name and birth date," Officer Brewer says. "I'll head over to Children's and get a read on the situation."

He leaves with my gratitude and my blood sample, and I am left with a fear so great that I feel physically sick. I can't rest, and I can't stop imagining Jacob on an operating table, surrounded by medical professionals whose job it is to save him from the mess his own mother created. I will myself not to look at the phone next to my bed because I know that as long as I'm staring at it, it won't ring. When it finally does, after what seems like an eternity, I jump and reach for it, desperate to hear a familiar voice.

"Mom?"

"Enid! How's Jake?" My heart races, and my hands shake.

"He's sleeping. His doctor said he'll probably sleep for a long time, so Mrs. Abbott brought me home to pick up some things."

"You're at home?"

"Yes, they said it was a good time to let Jake rest."

Relief washes over me. Jacob is *resting*! "Did he have surgery?"

"No, and the doctor thinks he won't have to. They gave him something to sedate him so he wouldn't freak out from the pain or from being in the hospital." Something clinks loudly in the background. "I think he'll like it okay there when he wakes up, though. There's a huge mural of Clifford on the wall in his room, if you can believe it." Another loud clink, this time like glass breaking.

"That's great," I say. "What's that noise?"

"I came in to get some of Jake's things"—her voice is tired and unemotional—"and I found your mess. I'm cleaning it up." More glass clinks, and I pick out the strangely familiar sound of a bag of trash being tossed into the receptacle in our garage.

"What mess?"

"The empty vodka bottle on the kitchen counter and the partial bottle and empty glass on the coffee table. *That* mess. The usual mess." Her voice echoes off the walls of the empty garage. A door slams.

"Not really much of a mess," I say. "A bottle and a glass."

"Mom, were you drunk last night?"

"Excuse me?"

"How much did you have to drink?"

I imagine Debbie Abbott standing in my kitchen, her arms folded judgmentally in front of her while she listens to my daughter make accusations. "Is she in the room with you?"

"Who, Mrs. Abbott? No, she's waiting in the car."

I don't say anything, trying desperately to think about what I can possibly say to allay Enid's suspicions.

"Are you afraid she'll see it, Mom?"

"See what, Enid?"

"I'm not stupid."

I wait for her to say more, but she doesn't. I take a deep breath and try to sound like the responsible mother I'm supposed to be. "I am an adult, Enid. I'm allowed to have a drink once in a while."

"Looks like you had a little more than *a* drink last night, and once in a while is a joke."

"How would you even know how much I had last night?" I can't believe the words as they fall out of my mouth. I'm engaging in an argument with a child over how much alcohol I consumed, and it's too late now to stop it. I should never have answered her first question.

When Enid speaks again, her voice is barely a whisper. "Mom, you're not very good at hiding it. I can't tell you how many times I've found you on the couch, passed out . . . and that *cup*, Mom. You never go anywhere without it."

I ignore that last part. "I wasn't planning on going anywhere last night, Enid! I had no idea I was going to have to come get you. I knew it was a bad idea, but I didn't know what else to do."

"So you admit it?"

"That I had more than one drink last night? Yes," I say, knowing I have to be somewhat honest right now.

"What about all the other nights?"

I think about the nights—and the days—and how much time I've spent in a numb, partially conscious state. I think about the times a little part of my brain has tried to tell me I've overdone it, and I've paid it no attention. Enid cannot know the whole truth. She will never trust me again.

"No," I say, sounding halfway certain. "And never again." This part, at least, I hope to be true.

There's a long silence before Enid sighs. "I better go. I want to be there when Jake wakes up."

"Okay," I say. "Thank you for being there for your brother."

"Well, *someone* has to."

Her words break me. I'm the one who does everything for Jake. I bathe him, I feed him, and I try to make sure nothing upsets him *every single day*. But when push comes to shove, have I really been there for him the way a kid like Jacob needs a mother to be? Or do I resent him so much for being complicated that I've distanced myself emotionally from him altogether and have become unable to make good decisions on his behalf?

I lie in my hospital bed, blocking out every sound while I try to remember the feelings I once had for my children. I vaguely recall watching each of them sleep in their cribs when they were tiny, when I was filled with such hope and amazed by what my body had been able to create. That was a long time ago, and for years now, I have been more focused on the difficulties they create. I honestly have no idea at what point I became so disconnected from them that I deemed them a burden that must be endured.

My nurse comes and goes, but I keep my eyes closed so I don't have to interact with her. I'm unjustifiably angry with her for taking my blood sample, even though I know she was just doing her job. At some point I drift off, unable to fight my exhaustion, and dream that I'm driving my car through a sandstorm in the desert, searching desperately for Jacob. I can't see in front of me even though my windshield wipers are on high speed, and suddenly the car jerks as though I've run over something. I jump out of the car, blocking my eyes to the billowing sand, and wake up, sweating.

I must have slept for hours, because when I wake, Stewart is here, sitting in a chair in the corner of the room with his eyes closed. His dress shirt is wrinkled, and the sleeves are rolled up. I watch him for a while before he stirs, opens his eyes, and notices I'm awake.

"Hey," he says, getting up and walking to my bedside.

"How did you get here so fast?"

"The company put me on the corporate jet. I guess it's good to be a big dog when there's an emergency." I try not to roll my eyes. "How are you feeling?"

All I can do is start to cry. He looks uncomfortable and rubs his hands together like they're cold.

"I'm sorry," I say. He reaches out to me after a long moment and pushes the hair from my forehead.

"It was an accident," he says, exhaling loudly. "Jake's doing okay. I went to Children's on my way here, and Enid is totally in control. Jacob was sleeping, so I thought I'd come check on you."

"I should not have been driving," I blurt out. He's going to know everything soon enough.

Stewart sits on the edge of my bed and crosses his arms. "I know."

"Did Enid tell you?"

"Yes, but to be honest, it wasn't a surprise. I figured that was the case before Enid started casting blame."

My cheeks burn, and I feel betrayed by both my daughter and my husband—her for telling on me and him for already suspecting the truth. "I didn't know I was going to have to rescue Enid. What would you expect me to do in that situation?"

He exhales again and holds his hands up in surrender. "Look, I didn't come here to accuse you of anything. This is my fault, too."

"Oh, really? How is it your fault, Stewart? You were thousands of miles away being a corporate mogul."

"*Stop.*" His face crumples, and I silently dare him to cry, but of course he doesn't. It occurs to me that in the nearly twenty years I've known Stewart, I've never seen him cry. "I know how you cope, Audrey. I've known for years, and I've let it go because I figured you had it under control. If you needed a few drinks to make yourself feel better, so be it."

I'm shocked to hear him say this. I thought it was so under control that it was a secret. I wash the cups, carefully dispose of the bottles, and freshen my breath. It's horrifying to think he's known and never said anything to me.

Anger floods through me. "How I cope? You mean how I cope with being stuck in an impossible situation?"

Stewart reaches for a tissue and dabs at the corners of his eyes like an old lady, which looks ridiculous since he's not really crying. It makes him look weak, which infuriates me further. "I shouldn't have ignored it," he says. "I should have talked to you about it and asked how I could help. I just didn't know if you really wanted my help, or if you did, whether I'd be able to give it to you."

"Did you tell our daughter you knew? And you let it happen anyway? The police took a blood sample!"

His head snaps up, and he grips the tissue tightly. "What? When?"

"A few hours ago. Stewart, I caused an accident! I could have killed our son and the driver of the van I hit. I *did* kill our dog. Jacob will never forgive me."

"Jacob won't really understand," he says, shaking his head. "He'll eventually forget."

"You don't know what he'll understand or forget! You don't know him well enough to say that." It's cruel and unfair, but I'm not wrong.

"Audrey, maybe there's a way to handle this. The fact is that you were unexpectedly driving in the rain in the middle of the night to get Enid. They know what her friends did to her." He lowers his voice as the nurse comes in, her pink Nikes squeaking on the tile floor.

The nurse cheerfully informs us that I should be able to go home in the morning. My stomach turns at the thought of seeing my children tomorrow and facing the damage I've done to Jacob. As she leaves the room again, my dinner tray is carried in, and I have to suppress the thought that I'd give my left arm for a glass of wine instead of the lukewarm baked chicken and potatoes on the plate.

Stewart stares at me silently while I push the food around with a fork, then stands, announcing that he's going to go back to Jacob and Enid. I'm alone again with my thoughts, alternately angry with myself for being so stupid and careless and with my family for allowing me to be so stupid and careless.

CHAPTER FOURTEEN

The nurse can tell I'm agitated, so she gives me a pill that she says will settle me down. It has a similar effect as a glass or two of wine, and before long I'm breathing evenly and feel almost in control again, surprised when Debbie Abbott peeks through the door and walks into the room.

"Hey," I say, my voice mellow.

"I hope I'm not disturbing you. The nurse said I can't stay long, but I wanted to see you." She clutches her Louis Vuitton purse in front of her chest.

"Sure. Want to sit down? How are the kids?"

"They're good. Well, better, at least. Jacob's doctor says he's going to be just fine. There was some internal bleeding, but they believe it will heal without surgery. Of course they are watching him *very* carefully." She rambles on nervously as she perches on the edge of the chair, which I notice for the first time is upholstered in material the color of vomit. "You probably know all this already."

"Thank you for being there for them," I say. "I hate being here, where I can't do anything."

Debbie begins to shake, and tears stream down her cheeks. "I feel responsible for all this. I thought I was being so smart to put the girls' phones in a basket in the kitchen, but I should have locked them up. I thought my party idea was so darn cute that I got completely swept up in it and didn't listen when you told me about the boys." She is hysterical now. "I was blind to who Kara had become right under my nose, and I'm so sorry for what she did to Enid!"

"What are you talking about? What did she *do* to Enid?"

"Kara is the one who took Enid's phone from the basket. *She* took the picture while Enid was changing into her pajamas. *Kara* sent it to one of the boys, and she probably knew what he'd do with it. I'm so disgusted with her I can't even look at her. Honestly, it's been a blessing for me to be at the hospital with your kids so I don't have to deal with Kara. Bob has spent the entire day calling parents and has even gotten the police and the IT department at his company involved to try to keep the picture from spreading further. I'm just so sorry, Audrey." She covers her face, now red and puffy.

"It's okay," I hear myself say, the words belying the blameful thoughts in my head. Enid may have started things with Kara by telling that Chris boy that Kara liked him, but Kara crossed a line. Kara did damage that will no doubt affect Enid's reputation and her future. I could probably press charges against Kara for child pornography and further distance myself from responsibility. I could do a lot of things, but I probably won't.

Debbie blows her nose. "If you hadn't had to come get Enid in the middle of the night, this would not have happened," she says with a wide sweep of her arm. The rational part of my brain knows she's only partially right—this or something like it would have happened at some point, and the outcome could have been even worse—but I don't want to shoulder the blame by myself. I think the weight of it will kill me, so if Debbie and Stewart want to take some of the heat, I'm not about to stop them. I've been trying to operate without support from family or friends for a long time and failed miserably. Let the people who have failed *me* feel bad, too.

"It's not okay, Audrey, it's really not," she adds, shaking her head as if trying to force thoughts out of it. I see something familiar in her face, in her eyes. It's the same thing I saw when I looked at myself in the mirror earlier. Self-doubt has a definite look to it, and I think Debbie may have more experience in this area than I'd ever have guessed. I neglect Enid to deal with Jacob and I pay for it, but maybe Debbie neglects Kara, too. We give our kids so wide a berth that we don't know what's going on with them. Kids don't act out and intentionally hurt their friends unless they are feeling hurt, too. Neither do adults, for that matter. Self-doubt becomes self-hatred before you know what hit you.

I sit and wait while Debbie composes herself. Within moments, she has neatly wiped away the smeared eye makeup and looks pretty again. I want so badly to hate her and her styled hair, shellacked fingernails, and designer clothes, but beneath the surface we're probably much more alike than different.

"Do you ever wish things had turned out differently?" I ask her, my voice barely a whisper.

"Oh yes," she says, her highlighted auburn hair bouncing as she nods to punctuate the words. "I should have known a sleepover wasn't the best idea. I wonder now if the party was really for me, not for the girls. Bob says I live vicariously through Kara . . ."

"Not the party. I mean things, life, *kids*." As soon as I say it, I wish I could rewind to thirty seconds ago and not open my mouth.

"Oh," Debbie says. "Sure I do, sometimes. I wish I'd paid more attention to what was going on with my own daughter. This technology is going to be my undoing!"

I'm flustered that she isn't picking up on the thing I'm trying to get at. I try to be more direct. "Where was

Thomas on Saturday? I didn't see him when I dropped Enid off."

She smiles proudly and fusses with a diamond bracelet on her right wrist. "He was at a sleepover, too."

It hurts to hear this, and pangs of jealousy tug at me. I want to hate her for this, too. Thomas and Jacob can't ever be put in the same category if Thomas has friends who invite him to spend the night. It's been years since Jake has even been asked over to play with someone for an hour.

My silence must be telling, because Debbie's face reddens, and her smile disappears. "I'm sorry. I know how that must sound to you."

She has no idea how it sounds to me. It makes me sad and angry, but it also makes me resent my own child yet again for not being just a little bit less . . . different, sensitive, inflexible. Does she know how it feels to wish she'd stopped at one child, or better yet, never had any to begin with?

"Enid says Thomas is really smart," I say, just to fill the silence. It sounds accusatory.

"He is, but it can border on obsessive when he gets interested in something new. Right now he's obsessed with airplanes, and Bob and I take turns driving him to the little municipal airport *every single weekend* so he can sit by the fence and watch the planes take off and land." She pulls on an earring, a huge, sparkling diamond stud. I wonder if Bob gave her the earrings for her birthday or their anniversary. Stewart hasn't given me jewelry since we got married.

"Sometimes I want to jump on one of those planes, just choose one at random, hop on, and go somewhere new," she goes on. "Someplace nobody knows me, and no one will find me. I'd get a job in a coffee shop or something and just blend in."

I'm surprised to hear this coming from a woman whose life seems so perfect. Maybe she understood what I was trying to say after all.

"I thought I was the only one who had those dreams," I say with a laugh. "You always seem to have it together, and I always feel like I'm falling apart."

"I work hard at faking it a lot of the time, and Bob rewards me generously for having a good attitude." She holds her hands out and wiggles her fingers so her rings and bracelets shine. "I'm spoiled rotten, Audrey, which makes it a little easier to put up with. My mother worked two jobs when I was a kid, so I consider myself lucky, but I do wish it could be different once in a while."

"How do you cope?" I ask, choosing a word Stewart used earlier.

Her eyes light up. "Well, I used to shop. Every day I'd get the kids off to school and go spend money. I was constantly redecorating my house and buying new clothes— for me and for the kids. We were the best dressed family in town!" I watch as the light disappears, the corners of her eyes sagging with the weight of her admission.

"But then Bob threatened to take my credit cards away, and I got bored with it, anyway. I was depressed for a while, but a friend told me she'd been taking anti-depressants with some success, and my doctor thought it was a great idea." She chuckles. "I never thought I was the type to take happy pills, but they really are great. See?" She smiles manically and pokes at her cheeks with perfectly polished fingers.

I can't help but laugh at her, and she relaxes, smiling naturally again. "Please don't take this the wrong way— I know you have bigger challenges with Jacob than I do with Thomas, that he depends on you so heavily and all—but sometimes I think it's worse that Thomas appears so normal at first glance."

"You're crazy," I say, pulling the pillow lower behind me so I can sit up straighter. My ribs cry out in pain, and I squeeze my eyes shut until it subsides.

"Are you okay?" She sounds legitimately concerned.

"Yes, I just forgot for a second why I'm in this bed."

"Do you want me to call the nurse?"

"No, I want you to explain what you just said. You wish Thomas didn't seem so normal? I wish the opposite about Jake a hundred times a day."

The nurse comes in and tells us it's time to wrap it up. Debbie stands and picks up her purse, but I'm not about to let her walk out the door until she clarifies what she just said. She stands right next to me and puts her warm, soft hand on mine.

"When people see Jacob, something about him communicates his differences. I think it prepares people for whatever might happen and immediately creates empathy for you. I hate the way this is going to sound, but people give him—and you—a wide berth." She waits for me to object, but I don't, the feel of her hand on mine reminding me we are connected, though I've often fought it.

"Thomas is viewed as just a regular kid until he gets worked up about something, like leaving the airport after three hours of watching planes or having to stop working on a project in technology club when the teacher says time is up. He almost fits in . . . until suddenly he doesn't. And since people aren't necessarily expecting it from Thomas, it's inconvenient and annoying to them. And horribly embarrassing to me."

I turn my hand underneath Debbie's so our palms touch. "I'm sorry," I say, a blanket statement for all the things I should apologize to her for—for envying her and pitying myself more for it. "I had no idea you felt that way."

"Well," she says abruptly, "I guess I'll go now, but I had to come see you and tell you face-to-face how sorry I am about what happened. Bob's not going to rest until he feels like the problem Kara created has been handled properly. I know you and Jacob have a lot of healing to do, too, and I will be here for you if you need me. Let me be that friend you can call when you need dinner brought over or carpools run. Just let me be that person. It's the least I can do for you." Her eyes are watery again, and it's as sincere as I've ever known Debbie to be.

I nod, though I know it's unlikely I will call her. I have changed my perception of Debbie and the challenges she faces, but I don't want what happened in the last twenty-four hours to be what bonds us.

CHAPTER FIFTEEN

As soon as I'm released from the hospital I go straight to the children's hospital. I try to encourage Enid to go home and rest but she refuses, so we sit in silence and watch him sleep. If he opens his eyes we jump from our chairs and ask him questions he can't answer, like, "How are you feeling?" or "Can I get you something? Water? Jello?" He's being kept on a mild sedative because the sounds, chaos, and bright colors of the children's hospital agitate him. They agitate me, too, but every time I look at my bruised, battered son, I know I deserve much worse.

Stuart comes every day bringing clothes for us both and Starbucks for Enid. I watch her cling to the white paper cup and think about my "A" cup. I'd do anything for a drink but it's what got me here, so I suppress the thought.

The relief I need during this dark time is a call Stewart receives from the police department. Apparently Officer Brewer had to respond to an emergency on his way back to the precinct to drop my blood sample off, and during the stop, several items were stolen from his patrol car, including my sample. The plumbing company did not press charges, and my insurance is taking care of everything, so it appears that legally I am going to get away with what I did. Stewart tells me I am getting a well-deserved second chance, though I think he says that to make himself feel like less of an accessory. I'm relieved, but I can't say I feel better at all. The guilt that has settled in the pit of my stomach like a rock isn't going anywhere.

<hr />

After an agonizing five days, Jacob is finally discharged. Stewart walks into the room fresh and polished, looking like a million bucks. I've taken a couple of showers in the hospital room, but my bruises have turned a horrid yellowish-green, my hair is matted to the sides of my head, and I smell like antiseptic. Enid has bags under her eyes, and I think it will take her a month to catch up on sleep.

"Ready, guys?" Stewart asks, sounding unnaturally chipper. An orderly has come in to help Jake into a wheelchair, and I have his personal items in a plastic bag on the bed.

"Ready!" I chirp back, attempting to match his enthusiasm.

We head down the hallway and climb into the elevator together. Stewart's aftershave is strong and smells out of place in the small, sterile space. The orderly kindly tells Jake that he's excited for him to go home, but Jake doesn't respond or even change the expression on his face. I'm glad the orderly is behind the wheelchair and can't see it.

When we get to the lobby, Stewart hurries ahead to unlock his car—mine was totaled in the accident—which is parked illegally along the curb. We lift Jake into a new car seat and buckle him in, all of us fussing over him, and pull out of the hospital parking lot.

"I have a surprise for you waiting at home," Stewart says, I'm not sure to whom.

"A surprise for Jake?" Enid asks.

"I guess it's for all of you, but mostly for Mom."

I turn to look at his profile. He glances at me quickly before returning his gaze to the road. He seems nervous all of a sudden.

"What kind of surprise?" I hate surprises.

"If I tell you, it won't be a surprise anymore."

"Telling me there's a surprise is enough of a surprise," I say. "Please tell me what I'm going home to."

He sighs. The kids are silent in the back seat. "Your sister is here for a few days."

"Jane?" I ask.

"Do you have another sister I don't know about?" Stewart jokes.

"Why is she here?" Even if I didn't hate surprises, I'd hate this one.

Stewart stares straight ahead as I glare at him. "You can't think I wouldn't call Jane to tell her about what happened. I knew you wouldn't call her, but she deserved to know."

Jane and I have not spoken since she called to share her concerns about Enid. A sick feeling washes over me as I recall that conversation and imagine the *I told you so* I'm going to get from her in person the minute I walk through the door of my own home.

"Tell me she didn't bring the husband," I say, pushing the thought from my mind.

"No, she came alone. It doesn't sound like things are particularly good between them right now."

"Shocker," I say.

"Mom, that's rude," Enid scolds. I ignore her.

Stewart makes an exasperated sound like air being let out of a balloon. "It was her idea to come. She wanted to come as soon as we talked, but I told her to wait until we knew when Jake would be coming home." We stop at a traffic light, and he turns toward me. "She was worried sick when I told her about the accident." He stresses the word *accident,* as if to assure me that Jane is none the wiser about why it happened. "Be nice, Audrey, and let her help."

I know there's nothing I can say about it. Jane is at our house, waiting for us to arrive. I stare out the window for the rest of the drive home, wishing I had a drink in my hand to help settle me down before we get there.

Jane is, admittedly, helpful to have around. She worked at an Italian restaurant for a few years in her thirties and throws together a beautiful pasta casserole for dinner from things she finds in my pantry and freezer. She tries to hide her disappointment when Stewart and I are the only ones to sit down and eat it, but Enid has disappeared to her room, and Jake is tucked under a blanket on the couch where we can keep an eye on him. He's still lethargic and has spent the last hour staring at the spot on the floor where Bud always used to lie.

Jane keeps the conversation afloat, carefully avoiding any talk of the accident or her own personal life. She asks Stewart about work, at which point I tune the whole thing out. I don't need to hear him drone on about how great his job is when everything sucks here.

I excuse myself to get started on the past week's worth of laundry, recoiling when I see the pajamas I bought Enid for the sleepover at the bottom of the pile. She was wearing them when the horrible picture of her started circulating and when she climbed into my ambulance that night. I wad them up and walk out to the garage, where I shove them into the big, rolling trash can. I never want to see them again.

Back in the laundry room, I get a load of wash started before I work up the nerve to open the cabinet. I feel like I'm opening a tomb, stale air escaping as it's opened for the first time in nearly a week. I push carpet samples out of the way, reaching to grab one of the bottles that have been so patiently waiting for me, promising myself I'll just take a few sips and put it back. I wave my hand around in the darkness, but there is nothing there. My heart sinks. Stewart must have found them and thrown them out. I hurry back out to the garage, where I think I may have a bottle hidden inside a box of Christmas decorations, but there is nothing there, either.

Jane is at the sink rinsing dishes when I walk back into the kitchen. I open the refrigerator and the pantry, hoping to find a partial bottle of wine or some Kahlúa I'd bought for a dessert I planned to make but never did . . . *anything*. There is nothing. Every trace of booze appears to have been removed from the house.

"Need help finding something?" Jane asks over her shoulder. I can hear the television in the next room. Stewart must have turned it on, but it sounds like some kind of sporting event. Not anything Jake will be happy watching.

"No," I say, keeping my voice low. "I thought maybe there was a bottle of wine I could open for you, but I'm not finding one."

"That's okay. I don't need any. Do you have any decaf coffee we could put on?"

"We don't have a coffee maker," I tell her. "Sorry."

"Are you serious? What do you drink in the mornings?"

I feel a pang of shame. "*Not coffee*," I say defensively.

"Okay, then," Jane says, holding up her hands in surrender. "Not coffee."

"I'm going to check on Jacob," I say, an easy excuse to leave the room, but Jane follows me.

Jake is sound asleep, and Stewart is nowhere to be found even though a football game still flickers on the TV. I turn the volume down and sit at the end of the couch near Jake's feet. I touch him, feeling his warmth through the blanket, and Jane settles onto the love seat across from us.

"So how are you feeling?" my sister asks.

My left leg bounces involuntarily, nervous energy inside me finding an outlet. "Fine. Glad to have Jacob home."

"Thank goodness for that," Jane says, smiling at her only nephew, who, still and quiet, is so easy to love.

"How long are you staying?"

"Ready to get rid of me already?" Jane raises her eyebrows at me.

"No, of course not. I just wondered how long we get to have you here. It's nice having someone who cooks in the house."

Even though we aren't close, Jane has a way of looking right through me like only a sister can, her eyes boring into mine like lasers. I look away, my hands suddenly freezing cold. I wring them together and tuck them underneath my legs, both of which are bouncing now.

Not wanting to be the only uncomfortable one in the room, I go for a low blow. "How's Mike?"

She frowns. "*Mick* is fine." She rubs her temples with her fingertips. "Actually, I take it back. Mick is an asshole."

"Oh, sorry," I say, though I am not sorry in the least.

"Whatever," Jane says, shrugging it off. "I don't want to talk about him."

It's quiet for a minute or two before she speaks again. "Do you ever wonder what it would have been like if Mom and Dad hadn't died?" The randomness and directness of her question are startling.

"I stopped wondering that a long time ago."

"Maybe because you're living it, Audrey."

"Excuse me?"

"Maybe if our parents hadn't died, you or I would have ended up where he is right now." She motions toward Jake.

"What are you talking about?" I have a sudden desire to get up and storm out of the room, but I'm frozen to my seat, my hands still pinned beneath my legs.

"I read an article recently that said children of addicts are up to eight times more likely to be addicts themselves." Underneath my legs, I extend my middle fingers at her. She can't see them and keeps talking.

"Dad was an alcoholic, Audrey. You probably don't remember, but I do. You were so little, but I was old enough to see it, and I remember when he'd make me take out the trash, the way the whiskey bottles sounded clanging around in the bottom of the metal garbage can." I look at her now, and the light from the television reflects back at me from the tears in her eyes. Jane was eleven when our parents died. I was only four.

Jane continues, "I used to think I could remember how Dad's cologne smelled, but I know now that what I remembered was the way booze smelled coming from his pores." I think about the smell I often remember of our mother and how it would feel to find out it wasn't her perfume after all. "I live with that same smell every day now."

I look at her, surprised. "Mick?"

Jane nods. "Did you know that if you're the child of an addict, you're usually either an addict yourself or in a relationship with one?"

"I'm sorry you married an alcoholic."

"Actually, I've married three."

"Wow. I guess I'm lucky Stewart doesn't drink much."

"You're completely missing the point I'm trying to make, Audrey. I think *you're* an alcoholic. I know what a person who needs a fix looks like. You can't sit still.

You've been searching for a drink all evening. I just think . . ."

"You just think you can show up after all this time and be my big sister again. The last time you left, all our money went with you."

"Lou was an addict. He branched out from drinking to doing drugs and stole from you to pay for them!" She keeps her voice low so as not to disturb Jake or attract Stewart's or Enid's attention, but her anger is clear. "That was humiliating to me, that my husband would do that to my own family, but people who can't admit they have a problem don't generally make the best decisions."

Jane looks at Jacob again, and I snap. "The only problem *I* have is people thinking they need to help me or fix me. I am not an alcoholic, Jane. I was at home— for the *night*, I thought—and had more to drink than I would have if I'd known I'd have to go pick up my daughter, who had been royally screwed over by her 'friends.' Stewart clearly put you up to having this conversation with me, but you can tell him I'm fine. I don't need him, I don't need you, and I don't *need* alcohol."

Jake stirs next to me and starts to whimper. I glare at my sister, indicating that our conversation is over.

━━◆ ◆━━

Jane and I barely speak for the next two days, and I fight back tears constantly. It's hard to differentiate my anger from the despair and anxiety I feel, but one thing I know for sure is that I am not in a good place. If I could walk away—just open the front door and never stop moving in the opposite direction—I would, but I feel so lost and despondent I can't even bring myself to make a plan. Besides, every move I make is being closely watched by Stewart, Enid, and Jane.

I call my doctor instead, make an appointment to talk about the antidepressants that seem to work so well for Debbie Abbott, and count the hours until my sister goes back to Montana tomorrow.

CHAPTER SIXTEEN

One thing I can say about antidepressants is that they haven't made me happy. Whose idea was it to call them happy pills, anyway? They might keep depression at bay, but they don't magically replace it with happiness. All my emotions are just dulled around the edges. I'm stuck in a fog, and I just don't care about anything anymore.

My house is a disaster. The sink is full of dirty dishes, and the refrigerator is full of food that should have been thrown out days ago. Enid has started doing her laundry and even some of Jake's when he runs out of blue shirts, because now all of a sudden, he refuses to wear green and I just can't bring myself to try to understand why.

Since the accident, he's back to being totally unpredictable, the way he was before we got Bud. If it's possible, he's even more irritable and prone to fits than before. The peace and calm that Bud brought into our home left the day I killed him.

I had Stuart put all Bud's things away before Jake came home from the hospital in the hopes that out of sight might mean out of mind, but yesterday he found a tennis ball under the couch that led to a house-wide search for Bud and a meltdown of such massive proportions that he ended up beating his head against the wall. Enid had to help me restrain him, which terrified her and absolutely wore me out. I lied and told Jake that Bud had to go away, back to his real family, and then sedated him with some medicine the doctor had given me when we left the hospital. He curled up on the living room floor in the place he used to lie with Bud and didn't move for six hours. All I could do was sit and watch him suffer, knowing I had done it to him.

Today I've gotten the basics done—fed the children breakfast, gotten them off to school on time—but now I'm exhausted. I can't remember when my last shower was, and, frankly, I don't care.

I'm sitting on the couch staring at the *Today Show* but not really watching it when Stewart comes out of our bedroom with a suitcase. He's wearing a shirt and tie for the first time since he came home three weeks ago. I vaguely remember him mentioning something about going back to Tokyo, but I somehow missed that it's happening today.

My mouth automatically unfolds into a smile, one thing the antidepressants have helped me do with ease. I smile on command all the time now, not because I'm happy, but because my face just does it without thinking. Nobody cares that I haven't done a single productive thing around here, because I *appear* to be fine and I haven't been drinking. Stewart sits beside me and folds his hands in his lap.

"I wish I didn't have to go back so soon," he says, but I know he can't wait to leave. I continue smiling as he reaches into his shirt pocket and pulls out a small silk drawstring bag, which he hands to me.

"What's this?" I ask, genuinely surprised.

"Just a little something. I know it hasn't been easy for you, getting over the accident and, you know . . ."

"Quitting drinking?" I finish for him.

He makes a face. "All of it. But Jacob is all better, you're all better, and our family is moving forward from that unpleasant situation." He makes it sound like we all had the flu or something.

I stare at the little bag in my hand. "Open it," Stewart encourages.

My fingers pull at the ribbon, though I am completely void of excitement as I tip the bag into my hand to reveal a delicate, gold charm bracelet. I hold it up to inspect the charms, two shiny circles, one with an *E* and one with a *J* engraved in the center. "It's pretty," I say.

"I thought you could wear this as a reminder of how important you are." He takes the bracelet from me and unclasps it. Like a starlet in an old film, I daintily hold out my hand so he can place it on my wrist.

"Thank you," I say, the reliable smile still plastered across my face even though the words that come out next are, "Don't go."

Stewart's smile mimics my own, but his is masking other feelings, too. *You know I'm not cut out for this parenting thing, but please, Audrey, don't screw it up this time. I don't want to come back here until I absolutely have to*, I can imagine him thinking.

"I have to go," he says. "I've been away from the project for so long." I raise my eyebrows, unable to convince my brain that a frown might be appropriate now. "Not that I minded being here at all," he adds, "but things are better, Jake's better, he's back at school, and I know you'll be fine."

He touches his lips to my forehead. It's not a kiss, just something he's been doing since the accident. It makes me feel fragile, like I'm a child. I want to scream and tell him that I'm not going to be fine and that he should not trust me enough to leave again, but the antidepressants hold the words back, and the corners of my mouth remain upturned, and Stewart has no clue that I'm more miserable now than ever.

"You can call me anytime. I'll have my phone with me no matter what." He reaches out to touch the bracelet one more time, picks up his suitcase, and disappears into the foyer. At some point his Uber must arrive, because I hear the front door open and close and then the house is silent again.

I stay on the couch for the rest of the day, watching disinterestedly as the shows change from morning TV to daytime drama, none of the content registering. I'm not hungry, and surprisingly, I don't want a drink. I'm numb, but in a completely different way from how I was when I drank. When I drank, I could still function. I haven't done a productive thing in days now that I'm "properly medicated," and each day productivity gets a little less . . . important to me.

When it's time to meet Jacob at the bus stop, I have to force myself to get up. My body is stiff. The aches and pains from the accident have gone away, so it must be because I haven't moved a muscle since Stewart walked out the door. I stop in the foyer and look at myself. I expect to see a tired, haggard woman looking back at me, but I look pretty decent. My unwashed hair looks shiny, not greasy, and the stress lines I'm used to seeing at the corners of my eyes and mouth have all but disappeared with the medicinally induced calmness. I look younger somehow, and I hate it. I want to look a hundred years old, because that's how old I feel.

I walk out of my house and wave at Mr. Burns as he pulls up to the curb and deposits the "precious cargo," as he refers to Jacob. Jake is smiling, content to be back in his routine; Mr. Burns is smiling, because he truly loves driving that damn bus; and I am smiling, because the pills help me do that without even trying.

Since I have done nothing noteworthy today, I make an effort to pay attention to Jacob for a while before Enid gets home. I sit and read two *Clifford* books aloud, though if asked what they were about, I wouldn't know. My brain tells my mouth what to say and when to turn the page, but the story is lost on me. Jake only says Bud's name twice during the stories, which is an improvement.

When it's time for *Gilligan's Island,* I turn on the television, but Jake no longer hums the theme song like he used to. Something makes me think of my mother, and I reach over to tousle his hair the way she used to tousle mine. My hand freezes above his head when I hear the bracelet Stewart gave me jingle from its place on my wrist. I stare at it, and thoughts of my mother are replaced by thoughts of Debbie Abbott. She told me about the gifts Bob gives her for putting up and shutting up. Is that what this bracelet is? Stewart said it's a reminder of how important I am, but the only initials on the bracelet are those of my children. Does that mean I'm not important to him? Or are the initials that dangle from the chain meant to serve as a reminder of what I almost lost, to keep me on the straight and narrow?

Suddenly it feels heavy, despite its delicateness. I unclasp it and yank it from my wrist, and it feels as if I'm freeing myself from handcuffs. I wonder if Debbie feels weighted down by all her reminders. We haven't spoken since the day she came to see me in my hospital room. She has left messages on my voice mail that I've responded to cheerfully via text message. *Got your message! Stewart is still home, and I don't need a thing! I've been trying some new recipes and find being in the kitchen therapeutic. Thanks for checking on us!* Total lies. Thank you, happy pills.

I knew I'd never really call her. I've been by myself for so long, and it's hard for me to accept help. I've become the martyr, though I've accused Stewart of acting like one, and I kind of like knowing that if I walked out of my house right now, lives would completely unravel. My kids may not realize it, but I am the center of their universe. I am the only person in the world who is truly responsible for them, even though I may do a terrible job of it. Besides, it was Debbie's daughter who did such an unspeakable thing to Enid. No matter how much I might want to like her knowing that her life isn't as great as it appears, she will always be Kara's mom.

I get up from the couch and walk to the garbage can in the kitchen. I step on the lever that opens the lid and stare at the bracelet in my hand before I drop it in, where it quickly disappears among the trash. I stare into the abyss of things discarded, expecting to feel a pang of guilt, but I don't.

CHAPTER SEVENTEEN

E nid missed a lot of school while Jake was in the hospital, refusing to leave his side. During that time,
Bob Abbott was able to do a lot of damage control regarding the photo Kara took of her, but since things
seen cannot be unseen, my daughter is still the topic
of tawdry conversation among a lot of kids at school.
Today, apparently, was one of those days, because the
front door opens with a crash that shakes the house and
slams again with equal force. Jacob, who is watching TV,
whimpers at the sound, and I move quickly to meet Enid
in the foyer before she brings her fury farther inside.
Her shoulders are hunched, and her face is twisted into
a scowl.

"Not a good day?" I ask.

"What's a good day, Mom?" she asks, throwing her backpack on the floor. "I can't even remember what one of those feels like."

"School stuff or people stuff?"

"Well, unfortunately there are people at school, so is it possible to separate the two?" She looks smaller than she did this morning, and her face seems to have absorbed all the lines and years that mine has lost. She looks like a forty-year-old with a child's body. She's been wearing baggy, oversize clothes lately and hasn't worn a bit of makeup in weeks, as if she's trying to let the clothes swallow her up so she can disappear into the background. I'm all too familiar with that feeling.

She stomps past me into the kitchen and rifles through the cupboards, slamming more doors before snatching a jar of peanut butter from a shelf. She wrenches the lid off and frowns at the empty silverware drawer. "Where are all the spoons?"

I reach into the pile of dishes in the sink, find a spoon, and squirt dish soap on it before rinsing it and handing it to Enid. She digs it into the peanut butter and shovels it into her mouth. Stunned by the sight of her eating something so fattening, I stand and watch as she scoops out another spoonful.

"What?" she asks when she realizes I'm staring at her. "I haven't eaten anything today."

"What about lunch?"

Enid snorts, licking the spoon clean. "I haven't been to lunch since I went back to school."

This is news to me. "Why not?"

"Seriously, Mom? There are five hundred people in the cafeteria at the same time. That's where all the talking happens, and I can't seem to walk by without someone saying something stupid and rude to me. Going to class is about all I can handle because the teachers don't let anyone talk, but the cafeteria's a free-for-all, so I just avoid it."

"Where do you go if you're not in the cafeteria?" I imagine her loitering in the school parking lot, smoking cigarettes with the outcasts.

Enid swallows, the smell of peanuts hot on her breath. "My guidance counselor's office. Nobody ever goes there except weird kids, and Mrs. Franklin is always at her desk just waiting to be needed. She's nice and easy to talk to, and I know she won't tell anyone what we talk about. It's, like, against her job code or something." I want to know what she and the counselor talk about, but Enid saves me the trouble.

"I told her about the picture, but she already knew all about it. Mr. Abbott did a decent job of making sure everyone knew it was taken without my knowledge, but nobody's really blaming Kara for it, either." She cradles the peanut butter in her arms like it's a baby. "Somehow I'm still the whore as far as anyone is concerned." I wince at the word and want to tell her not to speak that way of herself, but it would be like someone telling me not to think of myself as a loser right now, so I stay quiet.

"Someone hung a poster on the wall at school today that said, *Vote Enid Anderson for President of the* Small *Business Club.*" It takes a moment for me to understand what that means, and I'm horrified that anyone would go to that length to continue to harass Enid.

"That's it," I say. "I'm calling the school. There's no reason this should be allowed to happen . . ."

"Mrs. Franklin took the poster down, but she can't punish anyone because she doesn't know who put it up."

My cheeks feel warm, but I'm able to control my emotions thanks to the antidepressants. "I just don't understand how they can expect you to coexist in that building all day with Kara and *that boy*. They're both criminals as far as I'm concerned. Surely there's a *law* against that sort of thing!"

"Mom, stop. There's nothing the school can do because the 'incident' happened off school property on a weekend." Her nose is running, so she wipes it with the heel of her hand and then wipes her hand on her shirt. "Mrs. Franklin said all they can do legally is moderate, teach *responsible online behavior*, and keep it off campus."

"But it was *on* campus today!" My voice is loud but contained. Enid crumples, my outburst not helping.

She sets the peanut butter down noiselessly on the counter and slowly walks out of the kitchen. She looks every bit as helpless as I feel. I don't know what to do, and the only thing I can think of is to have a drink. I ignore the feeling tugging at me to follow Enid upstairs and instead scour my memory for anywhere I might have stashed alcohol in the past. I know the laundry room cabinets and garage are cleaned out, but there is a slim chance I stashed some away at some point and forgot where I put it.

Jacob is content on the couch watching TV, so I hurry to my bedroom and throw open the door of the walk-in closet. I search behind folded sweaters and inside two pairs of boots. I climb onto a step stool and pull old purses from high shelves, flinging them to the floor when they come up empty. Undeniably disappointed, I sit down on the stool and realize I'm sweating. I suddenly recognize that I need a drink more than I need to help Enid. I can't focus on anything beyond that. Just a small one will give me the clarity I'm looking for. I don't need more than that.

Almost as if by divine intervention, I see my suitcase, dusty and unused for the past several years, tucked away in the darkest corner of the closet, my long winter coat hanging down over it, almost obscuring it from view. I have a vague, disconnected memory of being on a flight with the kids—Enid was probably eight or nine at the time, which would mean Jacob was a baby—coming back from Stewart's mother's funeral in Ohio. Stewart stayed behind and helped "sort things out" and put me on a plane, alone, with our children. I remember that

Enid's ears wouldn't pop, so before long both of them were screaming and crying. A tiny bottle of Jim Beam appeared out of nowhere on my tray table. I think it must have been the gentleman sitting across the aisle, though he never took credit for it. It was an offering, I'd thought. *Here, take this. You'll feel better.* It was the beginning. I opened it, poured it into what was left of a clear plastic cup of watered-down Coke and melted ice, and polished it off in less than a minute.

The memory is starting to become clearer. When the flight attendant came back past, I asked her for two more. By the time she brought them, my insides felt warm, and the noise my kids were making didn't seem as bad, though I'm sure my fellow passengers would have disagreed. I slipped the little bottles into the side pocket of my carry-on bag for later and closed my eyes, surrendering to the things I couldn't control.

I jump from the stool and pull out the suitcase. Unzipping it, I am relieved to see that my carry-on is still tucked inside it the way I remembered putting them away. Jamming my hand into the pocket, I wrap my fingers around the treasures I had forgotten about years ago. The feel of them is like a salve to me and calms me enough that I take the time to put the suitcases away, just how they were, before locking myself in the bathroom.

I haven't had bourbon in years because the smell of it is too obvious. Right now, however, it's the cure for everything that's wrong with me, an antidote for the fact that Stewart is gone and my children and I are suffering. I twist the lid from the first bottle and let the fumes of six-year-old liquor fill the small space. I sip it slowly, the burning in my throat a welcome sensation. When it's empty, I lean against the sink and wait, breathing bourbon into my hand and then inhaling it again through my nose.

I know I can't drink the other bottle now, or there will be nothing left if I need it later. I pull a long piece of toilet paper from the roll and wrap the empty one up until it's just a wad of white paper, then stash it at the very bottom of the wastepaper basket. The other gets tucked under the sink behind a bottle of shower door cleaner. I take a deep breath and go upstairs to talk to Enid now that I can focus again.

I'm warm and tingly by the time I reach her door, and I have some idea of what I should say to her. What I *want* to say is that she should have listened to me—about the makeup and this new group of girls—but what I am going to say is that I'm sorry for what she's going through and empathize with how hard it must be to go to school and feel like everyone is looking at you and talking about you. I feel that way when I go places with Jake, which is why I don't go many places with Jake. At *his* school, being different is normal. At Enid's, fitting in and being like everyone else is paramount.

I tap on her door and don't get a response at first. I knock a little louder and lean into the crack between the door and the jamb. "Can I come in?" I ask, but in the close space, my breath comes right back to me, and the smell of bourbon is powerful. I should have brushed my teeth first. Enid is going to smell it and freak out.

"I just want to be alone." Her voice is muted, like she has her face buried in a pillow. I debate going in anyway but don't. Thankful I won't have to explain the booze on my breath, I head back downstairs to that tiny bottle waiting for me under the sink, deciding I need it now.

I savor this one as though it's an aperitif rather than a plastic bottle of fairly inexpensive liquor. I watch myself in the bathroom mirror as I drink, not sure if the pink flush on my cheeks is real or imagined, completely taken by surprise when Enid bursts into the bathroom, out of breath.

I try to wrap my fingers around the bottle, but there is nothing I can do to hide what I'm doing, and Enid snatches it out of my hand. She glares at me like I'm a bum on a street corner, minus the paper bag.

"Are you freaking kidding me?" she screams.

Just to prove a point—what point, I don't really know—I grab it back from her and tip the tiny bottle into my mouth to make sure I've gotten every drop.

"You're like the James Buchanan of parenting," Enid says, pointing an angry finger at me.

"What is that supposed to mean?" My tongue is tingly, and I have to think for a second who James Buchanan was.

"He was the worst president in US history." She crosses her arms while the comparison settles on me.

"Ah, so you're implying I'm the worst mother in history?" The words sting, and I stand up straighter, looming over her. "Well, he was elected by popular vote, so he must have done *something* right."

Enid smirks. "You're right, Mom. *He* was elected; parents aren't. I didn't choose you." She turns on her heel and walks out of the room. I want to run after her, screaming in my own defense that I didn't choose her, either, but I would be wrong. I *did* choose her, and I just let her down again. There is absolutely nothing I can say. I just watched the last shred of respect Enid may have had for me disappear.

Suddenly I wonder what in the world I'm doing. Did I really dig through unused luggage to find years-old bourbon? Was less than four ounces—barely enough to give me a proper buzz—worth completely alienating my daughter? I toss the bottle onto the vanity with a cheap, plastic clatter and run after Enid. I don't have to go far. She's standing in the middle of my bedroom with her face in her hands and spins around when she hears me approach.

"Screw you, Mom," she says through gritted teeth.

I'm nearly knocked off my feet by her words. "What did you say to me?"

"Unless that stuff makes you stupid *and* deaf, I think you probably heard me."

"Go to your room right now and stay there," I seethe. How dare she treat me like this? She doesn't move, and I've loosened up just enough to start making bad decisions. I lunge for her, knowing I'm strong enough to wrestle her to her room if I have to, but she doesn't move, doesn't flinch, and I almost knock her down with angry momentum. "I said, '*Go!*'"

Her face is completely void of emotion as she looks me right in the eyes. "I can't help you find your son if I'm in my room, since I'm pretty sure he's not there."

"What?"

"That's why I came barging in in the first place. The front door is wide open, and I can't find Jake. He's gone."

"And you're standing in my room? Waiting for *what?*"

Enid narrows her eyes. "I was trying to make a plan to go look for him! I was taking a second to *think!*"

"Oh my God," I say, shoving her out of the way and running for the door. A large rectangle of late afternoon sun lies on the foyer floor like a runway carpet, which I trample as I run out onto the front sidewalk. I stop and look both directions, thinking that Jacob cannot have gotten very far in such a short period of time, though I don't actually know how much time has passed since I last knew where he was. Worst-case scenarios flash through my mind, each one ending more tragically than the last, and none of which result in Jacob coming home to me.

"We should go on foot," Enid says from behind me. "He can't have gone far." At least I'm glad she thinks that, too.

I run next door, and Mrs. Speight answers after I knock frantically for what feels like minutes. She is in her robe and narrows her eyes when she sees me. "What can I do for you, Audrey?"

"Is Jacob here?" I ask, breathing hard.

"Why would he be here? You're out of breath, dear. Would you like to come in and sit?"

"No, I can't. Jacob left the house, and we don't know where he is. I thought he might have come here to see Reuben."

She shakes her head. "Reuben's not feeling too well today, I'm afraid, but Jacob isn't here." She looks over my shoulder and up the street.

"I'm very sorry about Reuben," I say, though even to myself, it sounds rushed and insincere. I still find myself angry with her about not understanding Jacob or letting him pet her dog anymore. No wonder he didn't come here. "I hope he feels better soon," I say, backing away and jogging back down her front walk.

"Audrey," she says, and I stop in my tracks, "would you like me to come help you look for him?"

"That's very kind of you," I tell her, "but I think it's better if you would stay here, just in case he comes back."

"Of course," she says, and I take off down the street. I glance behind me once and see that she has sat down on her front steps, little pink slippers peeking out from under the hem of her robe, looking out for Jake. I start to run.

I run through my neighborhood and call Jacob's name until my voice begins to get hoarse and I can barely breathe. The bourbon I drank, followed by the sprinting and yelling, has made my stomach sour. I keep having sensible thoughts, like calling Stewart or the police, but I override them every time, knowing what I really need to do is find Jake before anyone else knows he's gone. I cannot imagine what might happen if the police know my recently hospitalized, unsupervised, autistic son wandered off, and Stewart will kill me. I already know Enid will never forgive me for this in addition to the myriad things I've already done.

The sunlight is starting to fade, and Jake should be at home watching television, waiting for his dinner to be served on his special plate, not roaming the streets alone. He has no skills to fend for himself, and I imagine him somewhere right now, terrified and shut down. I stop running and bend over with my hands on my knees. Hysteria begins to bubble up, and a tidal wave of shame washes over me. I was hiding in a bathroom drinking while Jacob just walked out the door. He is vulnerable with no way of protecting himself. I have let him down repeatedly and put him in a position where he has nobody to properly care for him.

I throw up in the street, bourbon and bile leaving a bitter, nasty taste as they exit my body. I feel worthless and sit down on the curb, burying my face in my hands as loud, racking sobs take over. My family is broken. All this time I've blamed it on Stewart, but I'm the one who's been here with the sole responsibility of caring for my children, and I'm the one who's screwed it up. After the accident I swore I was going to do better, but nothing has changed. My first thought is always of myself and how I can make *my* life less miserable. I have not understood until now that *I'm* the one making me miserable. How can I blame Stewart for not wanting to be here when it's not exactly a great place to be? How can I blame Enid for her drama when I've done nothing to help her manage it? And poor Jake. How can I blame him for a single thing when his challenges are so much greater than I will ever understand? I leave him in a room by himself so much of the time because I assume he would rather watch *Gilligan* or stare at the wall than be with me, but I haven't worked hard to connect with him in such a long time. I've self-medicated with alcohol so that I can't see clearly what a terrible, selfish person I have become. Even now, I'm sitting on a curb crying about my problems instead of doing something about them. Am I already giving up on finding my son?

I don't hear the footsteps approaching until two pairs of shoes appear in the space between my fingers. Wiping my eyes with the hem of my shirt, I look up, and it takes a moment for everything to sink in. Enid is smiling through tears, and clutching her hand is a bewildered-looking Jacob.

"Jake!" I yell, jumping up and wrapping my arms around my baby. He goes limp in my embrace, too tired to fuss about being hugged, so I hold on to him for longer than I ever have before. I kiss the top of his head, which smells sweaty, like a little boy, and inspect his face and hands for injury. Finally convinced he is okay, I turn to Enid, standing patiently beside her brother, still half-smiling, half-crying.

"Where did you find him?"

"The park. He was sitting on a bench, and some lady was about to call the police when I ran up. She seemed really upset that he was by himself, but I told her we were playing hide-and-seek and he just couldn't find me and gave up.

I breathe a sigh of relief and give her a grateful smile. She lied because she also knew what might happen if we didn't find Jake quickly. She might be furious with me, but she's still protecting us. "It never occurred to me to look at the park," I say. "I never take him there."

"Maybe you should start," Enid says. "He seemed kind of happy, actually."

Each of us takes hold of one of Jake's hands, and together we slowly make our way home. As we near our house, I see Mrs. Speight, still sitting on her front steps.

Every bit of anger I've ever held toward her dissipates, and I let go of Jake and walk over to her.

"We found him," I tell her as she smiles and waves at my children. "Thank you for keeping an eye out for him, especially when you have Reuben to look after."

She reaches for my hand and pats it. "I'm just glad it didn't take too long for you to find your boy. That's a scary feeling." I take a deep breath and nod. "You might want to keep a closer eye on Jacob, though," she adds. "Kids like that need careful supervision." I nod and force a smile before following my kids into our house, shaking my head at her remark but acknowledging for once that she's right.

Inside, Enid has settled Jacob on the couch and flips through the TV channels until Jake makes that unmistakable squeal that means he sees something he likes. I expect her to leave him and seek me out to berate me for my negligence but she stays beside him, close but not touching. I stand in the doorway, watching them from behind and wondering if they'd be better off without me. Were Jane and I better off without my parents? Was Grandmother better for us in the long run? Would my kids be better without me? Tears fill my eyes until the sight of my children becomes a blur and I leave the room, unable to bear what's becoming painfully clear.

CHAPTER EIGHTEEN

I stop drinking again for a few days. Every time the thought occurs to me that a drink will make whatever situation I happen to be in less painful, I remember how it felt the day Enid accused me of being the worst mother in history, and the frantic search for Jacob after I'd ignored him to throw back a few sips of Jim Beam while hiding in the bathroom.

I hoped that my conscious and very obvious effort to not drink might be rewarded—that life at our house would somehow improve dramatically—but I've been hurting my family for so long that my penance is far from being paid. Jacob's behavior has deteriorated significantly, and I can't quite figure out why. Maybe the fear and loneliness he felt wandering alone through the neighborhood caused him to regress, because he has been fidgety, more irritable than usual, more sensitive to sounds, light, and touch (especially *my* touch), and has started going to the bathroom in his pants. I received a call from his school asking that I keep him home until the "bathroom situation is remediated," since his classroom is not set up for "incontinent children" and he now poses a "significant health threat" to his teachers and classmates. I guess even a school like Jacob's has its limits.

Unfortunately this means that I have to touch him a lot more, essentially having to diaper an eight-year-old, sometimes with a bit of force, which often escalates into something of a wrestling match. I have been kicked, scratched, and reduced to tears on several occasions, but where once I'd have thrown back a few cocktails to make it more manageable, I repress the need to drink and wallow in the awfulness I deserve instead.

In contrast to Jacob, who is, for some undetermined amount of time, with me all day every day, Enid has become almost an apparition. She speaks to Jacob in quiet, hushed tones, always planting a tiny peck of a kiss on his forehead before disappearing to her room. She has not communicated with me at all, however, since we got Jake home from the park that day but relies on me to transport her back and forth to school each day, which I do in complete silence without making a fuss.

Today Jacob and I are waiting for her in the new SUV Stewart bought to replace my totaled one. It is a beast of a vehicle, with every safety feature known to man. Enid comes out of the house wearing her new uniform of too-large sweatshirt and baggy jeans, her hair hanging straight and lifeless around her pale, drawn face. She's barely eaten lately and I'm sure she's lost weight, though it's hard to tell how much since she's practically swimming in her clothes. Watching her climb into the car breaks my heart; she is so void of energy, and her old feisty sparkle is nonexistent. I would give anything to have one of our old, spirited fights, rather than watch her fade away.

I glance over as she pulls her hair aside to buckle her seat belt and catch sight of a bruise on the back of her neck. I reach out to see it better, and she recoils from me, leaning up against the window.

"What happened to your neck?"

"Nothing," she snaps. The first word she's spoken to me in two weeks is like music to my ears, despite its tone.

"That's not nothing. You have a bruise *around your neck*." I reach toward her again, and she pushes my hand away. As she does, the sleeve of her sweatshirt rides up, revealing a dark spot on her lower arm. I know it's going to piss her off, but I grab the fabric of her sleeve so I don't actually touch her and pull on it. There are multiple bruises on her arm, and when she goes limp now that I've seen them, I slide her other sleeve up to find more. She looks positively beaten.

"Enid, how did this happen?" My mind is spinning, trying to imagine how my child could be so battered unbeknownst to me. I have been paying attention. I have been listening to her silence and giving her space, assuming that's what she needs. But she is physically marred, and I had no idea.

"My God. I should take you to see a doctor."

"*No,*" she says sternly. "I'm fine. Just take me to school. I have a test first period." She pulls her sleeves back down over her hands and looks straight ahead out the windshield.

I'm dumbfounded. "Enid, that's not *fine.* How did you get those?"

"I slipped and fell down the stairs at school the other day." Her eyes dart in my direction for a second, judging my response to this. I don't buy it for a second but doubt that sitting here staring her down is going to help.

"I wish you'd told me," I say, just to appease her. "I might have taken you for X-rays. That was a heck of a fall from the looks of it."

"Mom, it's really fine. Can we just go now?" She bounces one leg impatiently.

"Are you sure?" I want to know what else she's hiding under those clothes, what other bruises she incurred during this alleged fall, but she will never agree to show me.

She answers with a curt nod, and I force myself to back out of the garage and drive, despite the leaden feeling in the pit of my stomach. When I pull in front of the school, she lets herself out without another word and seems to vanish into the throng of students filing through the doors. I watch until the car behind me impatiently honks its horn, wanting the line to continue moving like it's supposed to so life can continue moving forward like it should. Except that I feel my life has taken a sudden, screeching halt.

I pull forward but turn into the visitors' parking lot rather than continuing out onto the main street. I put my car in park and turn off the engine, trying to decide what to do next. Jacob is silent in the back seat, not the least bit aware of the fight I am having with myself in my mind. I know what I must do, but I also know it may drive Enid farther away, if that's even possible.

I wait until the flow of students entering the building has reduced to a slow trickle, unbuckle Jacob from his car seat, and walk into my daughter's high school, nervously holding my son's hand.

It's quieter than I expect inside the lobby as the last latecomers scramble down the hallways to class, a relief since I'm taking a chance bringing Jacob to such a busy, crowded place. We step up to the reception desk, and I'm nervous. The woman behind the counter hangs up the phone and looks at me expectantly.

"May I help you?" Her eyes look beady behind thick glasses, but she smiles, and I exhale.

"I'd like to see the guidance counselor, please," I say.

"Which one?" she asks.

I feel stupid that I didn't specify and have to rack my brain for a minute before I can recall the name of the one Enid said she has been talking to. "Mrs. Franklin, I think." Jake starts to squirm a little, but I give his hand a gentle squeeze, and thankfully he stops.

"Do you have an appointment?"

"No," I tell her and suddenly wonder if Jake and I are going to have to wait hours to talk to her. In hindsight, I should have called first, but now that I'm here, I have to do what my brain is telling me to do. Enid doesn't need space; she needs a mother.

"New student?" the woman inquires, peering over the counter at Jacob with a quizzical look on her face.

"Oh no," I say. "My daughter is a freshman, and Mrs. Franklin is her counselor. I need to talk with her because I have concerns that my child is being bullied." I say this last part louder than I intend, but it seems to snap the woman into action.

"Why don't you come through this door over here? We have some comfy chairs you can sit down in. I'll go see if Mrs. Franklin is in her office."

We enter the waiting area and park ourselves on a faux-leather armchair, Jake squeezing his body in next to mine, making it far less "comfy" than advertised. We are there for less than two minutes when the receptionist returns with a young, very tall, attractive woman dressed in a bright, patterned blouse and navy pants and heels.

She extends her hand to me and introduces herself as Rachel Franklin. I shake her hand, and when I give her my name, her eyes widen, and she makes a sweeping gesture with her arms, ushering Jacob and me down the hall to her office.

"It's very nice to meet you," she says, closing the door once we are all inside. Jake stands in the middle of the floor looking around the small room. "This must be Jacob."

"I'm sorry," I say. "I made a completely spontaneous decision to come in today. Jacob is out of school for a while, and I probably should have called first . . ." I watch as Jake notices an aquarium sitting on a table in the corner. He is drawn to it, transfixed, and walks over so that his nose touches the glass, just like he used to watch Reuben out our kitchen window.

"Don't apologize," Mrs. Franklin says. "I'm glad you're here, and Jacob is more than welcome, too. It looks like he'll be happy watching some fish swim for a bit. It can be very calming." She smiles at him and offers me a chair closer to her desk. I sit down, nervous. Rachel Franklin is not at all what I expected. When Enid told me about her, I envisioned an older, frumpy lady, but she is extremely polished and fashionably professional. Her office is neat and tidy, and the walls are covered in Dr. Seuss quotes about succeeding and being yourself that somehow seem to apply beautifully to the kids I imagine come through here to see her.

"So this is where Enid eats lunch these days," I begin. I wonder if she sits at the table near the fish, if they calm her, too.

Mrs. Franklin forces a smile. "For a little while she came during her lunch period, but I haven't seen her as much lately. How's she doing?"

"Not good," I say. "That's why I came today. Where is she eating lunch if not here? I know she's not eating in the cafeteria, not that she eats much of anything anymore . . ."

"Are you sure she's not eating in the cafeteria? I assumed that when she stopped coming here, she'd gone back to eating with her friends." She has a look of sincere concern on her face.

"I'm positive. Well, not that she's actually told me that, but being in the cafeteria was really hard for her, people were giving her a hard time . . ."

She nods. "I know. She shared that with me, but she seemed to indicate that things were getting better. There was an incident with a poster, but I can assure you that was handled immediately, and the custodial staff know there should be no posters hanging on school walls for any reason now that the student government election is over."

Thankful to actually know about the poster incident, I nod, too. "She did tell me about that, and I appreciate your help in the matter, but I don't think things are better with her friends. As a matter of fact, I don't

know that she is associating with *any* friends right now."
I look toward Jake, but he's still mesmerized by the fish
and the water that bubbles and gurgles inside the tank.

"Oh," Mrs. Franklin says, and the corners of her
mouth turn down. "I'm sorry to hear that. The last time
Enid came by, she said things were a lot better."

I think about the drive here today that prompted
my visit and shudder. "I think she says a lot of things are
okay when they're not." I tell her about the bruises on
Enid's neck and arms, and how when I asked her about
them, she made up a story about falling down the stairs.
Rachel's forehead creases even more, and she rubs her
temples when I finish talking.

She takes a long, deep breath and leans forward on
her desk, folding her hands on top of it. "So you think
her story about falling down the stairs is untrue?"

"Yes," I say. "I have two kids. I've seen bruises from
falling down stairs on knees, elbows, and heads, maybe,
but forearms and the back of her neck? No. It looks like
someone has grabbed her very aggressively. Maybe the
kids who have been picking on her are doing it."

"May I be frank, Mrs. Anderson?" Her blue eyes are
piercing.

"Of course. That's why I'm here. We need to solve
this problem."

"When Enid started coming to see me, she shared
that she was having some problems at home. She mentioned that Dad is away a lot and that Little Man over

there requires a lot of your attention." We both look at Jake, and I nod my head. "She told me that you and Jacob had been in a pretty serious accident." I'm suddenly very nervous.

"Yes," I say guardedly, "the night the photograph of Enid was taken. She called me and was absolutely hysterical, so I jumped in the car—with Jacob of course; I couldn't leave him at home alone. It was the middle of the night, it was raining, and I was in a panic to get to her." I can't stop myself as the words pour from my mouth.

"When I saw the bruises today, it occurred to me that maybe the kids who are continuing to harass her with the comments and the poster, and maybe even Kara Abbott, gave her the bruises." Mrs. Franklin shakes her head almost imperceptibly, but it's enough to fuel me.

"*Yes*," I press, "it has to be them. In the hallways between classes, stairwells, other unsupervised areas . . . maybe before and after school . . . they could be intimidating her or getting back at her for getting them in trouble." I stop short and let out an unintended laugh. "Not that any of them were given any real consequences for what they did."

Rachel Franklin waits patiently for me to finish. She looks at me with pity or sympathy, or perhaps both. When she speaks, her voice is very low and quiet.

"Mrs. Anderson, I understand your concerns, and I agree that the bruises must be investigated; however, I don't think they are being inflicted at school. The students who were in any way involved in the taking and sharing of that photo have been warned—in very clear terms—that they are not to speak to Enid or about Enid, nor are they to go anywhere near her while in this building."

"But they *do* talk!" I snap, and I see Jacob flinch in my peripheral vision. "Isn't that why she quit going to lunch?"

Mrs. Franklin sighs. "Kids talk. They gossip. Most of the things Enid heard were coming from students who were not involved but who knew about it. That's tough, and it puts us teachers and administrators in an impossible situation, but we can't monitor and punish every single remark." I am about to interrupt again when she holds her hand up as if to say, *"Not yet, it's still my turn."*

"The first time Enid came to see me, she told me about the photo and the text—which I had already been apprised of by the principal and Mr. Abbott—and the accident, which she was very upset about. I remember her saying more than once during that visit that she wished she could turn back time." She pauses and smiles. "Who hasn't said that a few times in their life, you know?" She clears her throat. "It wasn't until the second time Enid came to see me that she told me about the troubles at home. She told me confidentially that you had struck her during an argument."

She leans back in her chair as if to allow me a moment to absorb what she's just said. As her accusation settles on me, my anger boils over.

"I did not do that to Enid! I did not make those marks on her! How *dare* you suggest that I am manhandling my child at home while you dismiss the very good possibility that kids are targeting her here, on your watch!" Jacob whimpers from the corner, and Mrs. Franklin stands up and walks around her desk toward me. I stand up, too, grab Jake's arm, and head for the door, but the smell of feces hits me before I can storm out. Jacob has gone to the bathroom in his pants. I know Mrs. Franklin can smell it, too, but she comes closer anyway, reaching her hand out to me.

"Let me help you," she says.

It is all I can do not to rage against her. "How are *you* going to help me?" I scream, and a moment later, the door to her office opens, the concerned face of the receptionist appearing, asking if everything is okay.

"Can you please ask Nurse Carla to come and bring the full kit?" The door closes again, and still Mrs. Franklin stands before me, seemingly not angry or intimidated by my outburst. It occurs to me that the *full kit* might contain a Taser or stun gun or something and I'm about to get taken down, so I back away, sink into a chair, and start to cry. I can't even advocate for Enid without screwing it up.

When the door opens again, a sweet older woman with super short, white hair and brown surgical scrubs walks in carrying a large plastic bin. She exchanges a few whispered words with Mrs. Franklin before putting on rubber gloves and laying a plastic sheet on the floor in the middle of the room. She introduces herself to Jake as "Nurse Carla" and takes his hand, and I watch as I continue to sob as she somehow, amazingly, gets him to lie down on the sheet while she strips his pants off and cleans my soiled child. From the bin, she produces a pair of too big, too long scrub pants similar to her own, which she cinches at his waist with the drawstring and cuts the legs off with a pair of medical scissors so they are a proper length for Jake.

By the time she's finished, I'm in awe. Carla puts Jake's nasty pants and underwear in a plastic bag and folds the sheet and wet wipes up for disposal before pulling off her gloves and holding up a lollipop. "Mom?" she asks. "Would this be okay?"

I smile and tell her it would be fine. "How did you do that so easily?"

"We've got plenty of special kids of our own. We stay prepared for pretty much anything." She picks up the full kit, and I cross the room to hug her. She hugs me back, a warm, tight, maternal hug that I wish I could feel for the rest of the day. When Nurse Carla leaves the room, I blow my nose and face Mrs. Franklin.

"So much for trying to do the right thing," I say, half joking. "I feel like a child abuser, and my kid crapped his pants. I suppose I'll call it a day." I locate my purse and the bag with Jake's poopy pants inside and reach for my son, who looks homeless in cutoff scrub pants.

"I'm sorry," Rachel Franklin says sincerely. "I certainly didn't mean to accuse you of anything, but I had to bring it up. When a child tells me he or she has been hit by an adult, I have no choice . . ."

This time I hold up *my* hand to stop her. "Except that I didn't hit Enid. Thank you for doing your job, but she grossly exaggerated having a phone knocked out of her hand. I may be the worst mother in history—her words, not mine—but I don't hurt her. Physically," I add after the fact since I'm being honest. I am completely exhausted, and I just want to go home.

"I believe you, and I will continue to look into the situation. I promise, Mrs. Anderson, we will get to the bottom of this." She reaches out to shake my hand, but I have Jake by one hand and the bag of dirty clothes in the other, so I just force a smile and walk out. She follows me to the door out to the lobby and waves sadly as we go. Coming here today, I thought she was someone who could help me help Enid, and while perhaps she does care about the welfare of my child, Enid seems to have her own strange agenda against me. I cannot believe she told Mrs. Franklin I hit her, and I'm not sure I've ever felt so hurt before.

The hallways are eerily quiet as we leave the school building, and as we get into the car, I look back at the place where my daughter sits somewhere inside and wonder if my relationship with Enid is truly beyond repair.

CHAPTER NINETEEN

The entire way home I fight the urge to stop at a liquor store. I can imagine how comforting it would feel to drink myself into a coma right about now, to forget for just a little while that my daughter has lied intentionally to hurt me and make me look bad. I get goose bumps at the thought of becoming numb to what is most painful to me. Twice, I even turn onto roads that will take me past one of the many places I have bought booze in the past.

I don't know what keeps me from doing it—it's certainly not self-control, since I literally can't stop thinking about drinking, plus I'm angry and humiliated, which is usually what triggers the need for a drink—so

217

maybe it's guilt that keeps my foot on the accelerator and my hands steering toward home. Or maybe it's fear. If I drink again and get caught, what could happen? To Jacob, to Enid, and to me?

I put clean underwear and pants that fit on Jacob when we get home and read to him for a while. I know he's missing the routine of being in school, but after this morning, I realize he's taken so many steps backward, it will be a while before he can go back. He's like a toddler all over again, and I can't leave him for more than a few minutes now without worrying.

Today Jake wants to read *Curious George* instead of *Clifford,* so I read until I can't stand the insufferable little monkey anymore. I make Jacob lunch and watch him eat, oblivious to my bored stares, and settle him in front of the TV. I can't sit still anymore, so I set the alarm on the security system—my new way of ensuring that Jake doesn't leave the house without my knowledge—and go upstairs.

I open the door to Enid's room tentatively, as though she's in there and ready to scream at me to get out. She's definitely not the tidiest child, but I'm still taken aback by the messy condition of her room. Her comforter is on the floor, clothes are draped across every piece of furniture, and her desk is littered with books and papers to the point that I can't see the surface of it. Although I am guaranteeing a tantrum later on for invading her space, I make her bed, hang or fold clothes that appear to be clean, put dirty things into the hamper, and start to organize the things on her desk. I feel like a mother doing it. Mothers do things all the time without worrying about how their kids will react, but for some reason, I often *don't* do things because I fear the backlash I will get from Enid. Right now I feel ready for once to stand up to her when she inevitably gets angry. I will tell her I did it because I'm her mother, and that, in and of itself, is a good enough reason.

I actually start to look forward to standing up to Enid, and in my mind, I imagine the moment when she narrows her eyes and plants her fists on her hips, ready to go to battle. She can call me the James Buchanan of parenting or any other clever thing she can come up with, but I will be ready. "Not this time," I'll say. "I'm your mother, and I get to decide what's best for you." And I'll mean it.

As I arrange the books on Enid's desk from shortest to tallest, I come across a copy of *Catcher in the Rye* and hold it, remembering the day Jane called to tell me she was concerned about something she'd seen Enid post on Instagram that had to do with the book. The book feels strangely warm in my hand, as if someone had been reading it just moments earlier. I turn it over and see that it's heavily dog-eared.

Carrying it over to her bed, I sit on the edge of her Pottery Barn Teen comforter and flip through the pages. I read each page that she's folded the corner of, first thinking what a smart and clever girl Enid is to appreciate such a thought-provoking and deep novel, but as I continue reading, I'm overcome by sadness for Holden Caulfield. I haven't read the book since college when I wrote a paper on it for a Sociology class, but I had forgotten what a sad, lonely character he is. Holden wants to be independent more than anything because he sees the world as such a hostile and unwelcoming place.

Every page she's marked speaks of isolation and self-destruction. Is that why Enid wrote that she felt she could relate to Holden Caulfield? The thought breaks my heart, knowing that even more now than when she made that comment, she must feel so alone. Holden does not end up having anyone to truly depend on and only his younger sister whom he really seems to love. If that's not a parallel to Enid's life, I don't know what is.

I can totally see now why Enid would feel a connection to this character, though I wish it weren't the case. I grip the book tightly and wonder what's happened to my child and how much I've had to do with it. Probably more than I'd ever think.

I pace the house for a long time after I finish making Enid's room look welcoming again. I walk through the living room every few minutes to see Jacob still staring at the television, but I'm too preoccupied to interact with him. My thoughts are all over the place, wishing I could go back to a time when things in my house were better—they don't have to be perfect, for crying out loud, just *tolerable*—and I could stop feeling so miserable about everything.

I suddenly wish I'd stopped at a liquor store on the way home or even just picked up a bottle of wine, and I begin to hatch a plan that might allow me to find balance again. Everything in moderation, right? A couple of drinks a day, carefully spaced out and only when I'm completely alone, might be able to bring a sense of control back to my life. The trick is to be regimented, careful, and I will have to be sure nobody in my house ever finds out.

I can stop at a restaurant and have a drink at the bar or at a table out of the way. I can pay cash and chew gum as I leave. There will never be a shred of evidence, but it will be enough for me to feel like I've gotten some control back. I'm certain that's all it will take to make me sane again. I just have to get Jake back in school, I think, as I rush to the living room to check for clean, dry pants. I lift my son up to see a dark, wet spot on the couch cushion and swear under my breath as I carry him, squirming, upstairs to change his clothes.

CHAPTER TWENTY

"Thanks a freaking lot, Mom," Enid says viciously as she climbs into the car and pulls the door closed with a deafening clang.

"What did I do now?" I ask, though I am pretty sure I know exactly what she's so worked up about.

She looks out her window and shakes her head. "I missed half of third period and all of fourth sitting in Mrs. Franklin's office being interrogated."

I want to ask if Mrs. Franklin's office still smelled like a dirty diaper, but I hold my tongue. I seriously doubt her visit to Mrs. Franklin was any worse than mine. "What was the grand inquisition about?"

"As if you don't know."

Jacob is half-asleep in the back seat, so I keep my voice low. "Here's what I do know: You have awful-looking bruises on your neck and arms and lied to me about how they happened. I went to see the counselor you speak so highly of to share my concern that kids at school are giving you the bruises, only to find out that you told her I hit you." I stop talking while we sit at a traffic light, but as we start moving again, I continue. "Do you know how it feels to have it implied that perhaps *I* was the one giving you bruises?"

"Mom, why would you think anyone at school was hurting me? Nobody comes anywhere near me anymore. I'm like the walking plague." She sniffles, and I can tell she's started crying.

I think of the worn copy of *Catcher in the Rye* in her room and try to stay calm. "You still lied to your counselor. I have never hit you."

"Sometimes I feel like you're about to—like you want to." She folds her arms. "It seems like it's the same thing."

"Except that wanting to do something and actually doing it are very different," I say through clenched teeth. We drive the rest of the way home in silence, though I'm far from finished with Enid.

At home I fix Jacob a snack and settle him back in front of the TV. For someone who's supposed to be handling my child's education until he's properly potty trained again, I've done a poor job of it. My priority right now has to be Enid, though, and I promise myself that as soon as I get the situation with her under control, I will begin in earnest to engage Jake and get him back to school.

Enid has been in her room since the minute we walked in the door, so I work up the courage to be her mother who was so strong earlier and head upstairs. I knock on her door and wait patiently until she turns the lock and lets me in. Her room is still neat, but she makes no mention of how it got that way.

"I'm sorry I exaggerated to Mrs. Franklin," she begins before I have a chance to say anything. It feels like a familiar situation, and I realize it's exactly how she handled the fake Instagram account *and* when I took her cell phone and found she had tried to wipe it clean. Both times she was quick to apologize, and I see now that she knew an apology would make me back off because I would rather let go than stand up to her. Not this time.

"Enid, you didn't exaggerate. You lied."

Enid turns away from me and walks to the other side of the room. "I guess that makes two of us," she says.

"What?"

"Mom, you've been lying and covering stuff up for . . . forever! Why is it such a big deal when I do the same thing?"

"I'm not sure you understand the severity of what you told your counselor. I could be reported to Child Services if Mrs. Franklin believes you. I can be reported even if she doesn't—she may feel like she has to cover her ass regardless!" It's shocking to me that Enid can be so brilliant at times and yet behave with such stupidity at others. "I want to know how you got those bruises, and I want to know *now*."

She pulls up the sleeves of her baggy sweatshirt, and I'm shocked all over again to see the marks there. She balls up her right fist and begins to pound on her left arm, while I stand, speechless, not understanding why she's doing this. I feel stuck to the floor as I watch my daughter beat on herself and then change arms. Her eyes look blank and disconnected, but she keeps pounding. It's not until she wraps her hands around her own neck that I realize that Enid's bruises are self-inflicted, and I take three giant steps to reach her. I grab hold of her hands and wrestle her onto her bed.

"What are you doing to yourself?" I pin her arms down and stare into a face I no longer recognize. "You're hurting *yourself* and letting the blame fall elsewhere. I was ready to get some kids kicked out of school this morning, and someone could show up at our door any second to investigate me for alleged child abuse!"

She looks at me with disgust. "If it makes you feel better, I did tell Mrs. Franklin today that you didn't hit me."

"Enid, I'm not sure it does make me feel better to know you're doing this to yourself. Why in God's name?"

I let go of her, and she sits up a little, scooting back toward her pillows. She pulls her sleeves back down.

"It makes me hurt in a different way, I guess. By the way, I also told her about the accident."

I feel like we're going backward. "You told her about the accident weeks ago. She mentioned it today."

Enid looks at her hands, the same hands that have been doing such damage to her. "I told her more. Today I told her *why* it happened."

Involuntarily, my eyes widen, and my neck elongates. "You mean because I was driving fast in the rain to *come get you*?"

She looks at me through a wisp of hair that has fallen across her forehead. "There was a little more to it than that."

"Oh, there was a *lot* more to it than that," I say, louder than I mean to. "I may have had too much to drink that night, but I didn't think I'd have to go rescue my daughter from her idiot *friends*, who, for the record, I knew were idiots to begin with." As the tirade begins, it's almost as if the resolve I had to simply stand up to and be a mother to Enid is gone. In its place is now bitterness and contempt. I feel betrayed that she keeps wanting to blame this all on me, and the concern I felt for her earlier has been replaced with rage.

"You know, my biggest mistake that night was letting you go to a party where I knew you were on the bottom of the food chain, being dangled like bait to that boy who had no good intentions toward you. You set yourself up for humiliation!"

"You're right," she snaps, coming to a full sitting position and pulling her knees to her chest. "I did set myself up. I should have known there isn't a boy at school, much less a cute, popular one, who would look twice at me. I should have known there was no chance Kara Abbott and her popular friends would want to be friends with a loser like me . . . but at least I can admit it and talk to someone about it and take the blame. You messed up even bigger than I did, and you keep sweeping it under the rug like the whole thing was my fault!" She is shaking, and in my peripheral vision, I see Jake peering in from the hallway. At least he's not throwing a fit, too. I'll deal with him later.

"So you told your counselor that I was driving drunk the night of the accident? Maybe instead of Child Services, she can call the police. Then what, Enid? Who's going to take care of you and your brother if I'm not here? Your dad?" I'm spitting, and my throat is beginning to hurt from yelling.

"No!" she screams. "That's the problem! Dad doesn't care about any of us enough to stay, and you're a complete mess. There is nobody left to take care of Jake and me, and I can't do it all by myself. I'm a *child*, Mom! I tried hard to be grown up, which is why I wanted to fit in with Kara and her friends in the first place. They seemed mature, and when they liked me—or when I thought they did—and Ben started paying attention to me, it made me forget how awful everything else is."

I snort. "Yeah, they turned out to be super mature, didn't they?"

Enid looks at me with such sadness, her once sparkly brown eyes dull and lifeless, and when she speaks it's barely a whisper. "Like you said, I set myself up. I asked for this by trying to be someone I'm not. But I didn't ask for you to be my mother. I guess I'm just stuck with you."

"Poor Enid. Go tell your guidance counselor all about it."

"I did. I didn't just tell her you were drunk *that night*," Enid says, all the hard edges gone from her voice. "I told her you're an alcoholic."

It's a slap in the face, a label I've spent years carefully avoiding. My cheeks burn and my stomach lurches, and I want to smack her, but she's hurt herself enough. I turn and walk slowly out of the room while the shame of her accusation engulfs me. I am *not* an alcoholic. Drinking used to help me be here and *stay* here, and she should be grateful that at least one of her parents is, because it's the last place in the world I want to be right now.

Anger surges through me with a sharpness and clarity that is startling, and I'm not even sure whom it is I'm angry with anymore. I'm beginning to find it hard to breathe. I know of only one way to feel better, to come out of this horrible fog and stay out. Without thinking, I grab my purse and keys and jump into my car. I don't tell anyone I'm leaving. If I just go and come back, maybe it will look like I went for a drive to clear my head. I will go have a couple of drinks and come home with no evidence, just like I planned. I just want—no, I *need*—to feel like myself again. I know I can do it—and I will be more careful this time.

I back out of my garage slowly and pull out into the street, carefully sticking to the speed limit even though I have not had a drink yet. I stop for longer than I need to at stop signs and accelerate gently after red lights, like a model citizen. Even as I drive, I'm aware of what drinking has nearly cost me in the past, but I'm no good to anyone feeling the way I do right now.

It's been so long since I've been to a restaurant that I don't even know which one to pick, though whether the food is good or not is of no concern to me. As long as I can order a drink I'll be fine, and I'm not the least bit worried right now about who I'll run into.

I decide on a chain restaurant because it's close and I'll be able to get home quickly. It's early, and most people won't be coming in for dinner yet. I ask for a table just so I don't have to look at a bartender the whole time. The place is practically empty as I'm seated near a window, the closest patron three tables away and from the looks of it just starting his second beer.

I order a vodka tonic and ask for a menu, which is just for show since I have no plans to order anything else. The waiter returns with both in record time, and when I swallow the first sip, I shiver, and my shoulders relax. By the time I've finished my drink, the man nearby has ordered another beer, so I order another for myself. I suppose when you are alone at a restaurant in the late afternoon with a drink on the table, it's pretty clear why you've come. I will tip well and perhaps be judged accordingly.

As the waiter sets my second drink down and collects my empty glass, I tell him I've decided against ordering food, which doesn't seem to surprise or disappoint him in the least. He goes ahead and drops my check on the table, and I'm grateful I won't have to interact with him again.

I sip this drink more slowly and watch the cars pass on the street outside. Busy people are going places, taking kids to after-school activities perhaps or heading home from work to their waiting families. I think about my family: Enid, alone in her room, so alienated and despondent that she has started inflicting pain and injury on herself, and Jacob, whom I last saw standing outside his sister's room listening to us as we spoke so horribly to each other. I did not see Jake when I left the house. I didn't set the alarm when I left, either. God knows what he might have done if he heard me leave. He could have walked out the door like he did last time and be anywhere by now.

I jump up from the table, feeling sick as I throw money down. Speeding home, I wish I'd never left, and all I can ask myself the entire way is what I could possibly have been thinking. The last mile is painfully long, but I pull into my driveway and jump out of the car, relief filling me when I see that the front door is not hanging open, an indication that Jacob is most likely still inside.

Letting myself in, I pause and listen. I have not been gone that long, and with my car parked in the driveway, it could appear that I've been home for a while. It's nearly dinnertime, and I wonder if it's possible that Jake hasn't noticed my absence. Enid is probably in her room wishing she had a different mother, but that's fine. It's my job to fix that.

The sun is on its way down, and nobody has bothered to turn on any lights, so it's dim in the foyer. I can see the colors from the television screen bouncing off the wall in the living room, so I set my purse down in the kitchen and open and close a few drawers and cabinets, banging around a little so I don't startle Jacob.

When I look over the back of the sofa, though, he's not there. I reach for the remote and shut the TV off, listening again to my silent house. As I reach the bottom of the stairs, a muffled sound makes me stop short. Enid's voice travels down to where I am, and I freeze. She sounds like she's laughing, which is a relief to hear considering the shape I left her in. I'm sick again at the thought that I walked away from her instead of acting like a parent like I'd planned.

I creep up the stairs, trying to gauge whether it's a good idea to tap on her door, apologize, and smooth over what happened earlier. Her giggles are drawn-out and not punctuated by words, so I think she must be on the phone, though I wonder whom she could be talking to since she doesn't seem to have friends anymore. Regardless, it won't go over well if I barge in on a phone call, so I tiptoe past, avoiding the squeaky floorboard in the hallway, to Jacob's room.

I switch on the light expecting to find him hiding in his bed, scared to death if he was aware of my unannounced departure, but his room is empty, and his bed is still pristinely made from this morning. His bathroom is also vacant and undisturbed, so I start to worry. As I hurry back downstairs, Enid's giggles continue, and I'm almost back to the kitchen to scour the house for my son when I hear her squeal, "Jakey!"

I turn back and run, unable to remember the last time Jake was in his sister's room. I don't bother knocking, ready to defend my lack of courtesy as concern as I push open the door to Enid's bedroom.

Jacob is sitting cross-legged in the middle of the floor. He turns his head slightly when I enter but quickly returns his attention to Enid, who is sprawled on her back on the bed, her head hanging off one side, her face red as blood rushes to it. She has taken off her sweatshirt and wears only a tank top, the bruises on her nearly skeletal arms horrifying. Her laughter turns into a gurgle when she sees me.

"What up, Audrey?" she says. "Jake, look who's home!" She rolls over onto her stomach, kicking something off her mattress that then hits the carpet and rolls to a stop at my feet. It's a vodka bottle, the kind I used to buy.

"Where did you get that?"

"It's yours, silly! Remember when you were in the hospital? I didn't throw it *all* away," she says in a voice that sounds nothing like hers. I pick up the bottle, which is about half-full. "Don't worry; I left you some."

"How much have you had to drink, Enid?" I shout. She starts to giggle hysterically, and I grab her chin, the familiar smell coming off her breath nearly knocking me over. With our noses almost touching, I force her to look at me. When her eyes finally focus on mine, her lids droop. "How much?" I ask again.

"How much have *you* had?" she drawls.

"Two," I say, the truth easy this time, though I doubt she will remember.

"I've got some catching up to do, then," she laughs. "I've only had a half!" Her head falls to one side like it's too heavy for her neck to hold up, and I grab her face again.

I gasp, holding the bottle in front of her. "Was this full?"

"At some point it was," she says, her eyelids fluttering closed. "You know, I get it. I *totally* get why you drink. This stuff makes all the sad just . . . go away."

"Sit up!" I yell, which makes her flinch and pull her legs underneath her so she looks as though she's about to crawl off the bed. "You need to get it out of your body. Let's go to the bathroom and throw up."

Enid lifts a hand and grabs for the bottle. I yank it away and curse, forgetting that Jacob is sitting watching the whole thing. I glance at him, and his eyes are wide, riveted by his sister's strange behavior. "Stay here, Jake," I say, running from the room.

I'm breathing hard by the time I've retrieved my cell phone from the kitchen and dial 911 on my way back up the stairs. Enid is conscious, but I don't know if she will be for much longer. I think about what would happen to me if I drank that much that fast and shudder. Enid is barely ninety pounds.

I am surprisingly calm as I explain to the emergency operator what my child has done and give her our address, but when I hang up, my hands start to shake, and my eyes blur with tears. "Jacob, I need you to come with me," I say, scooping him up, forgetting until right this second how much he's grown recently, and hurry him to the kitchen in my arms. I sit him at the table with a juice box and hope he will stay there while I go back to get Enid.

Dizzy now, I take a deep breath before I loop one arm under Enid's legs and the other under her back, like a groom ushering his new wife over the threshold. She's becoming groggy, but I pepper her with questions to try to keep her alert.

"Why did you do this?" I ask finally, leaning her against the wall on the bottom step while I open the front door to await the ambulance.

She mumbles something, and I lean in and ask her again. It takes great effort for her to open her eyes all the way, but when she does, there is such sadness within them. "I wanted you to know how much it sucks to be us."

I choke back tears and hold her up, whispering that everything is going to be okay, that we are going to go to the hospital and get her better. I tell her for the first time in so long that I love her. "Don't be like me," I plead. "You are already so much better." Tears make their way down my cheeks, and my nose runs, but I don't dare let go to wipe my dripping face.

A police car arrives first, and I have to repeat everything I told the operator a few minutes ago. I hold my daughter tight and cry while he asks more questions. *Where did she get the alcohol? Was it locked up? Do you know if this is habitual behavior?*

The ambulance finally pulls up in front of the house, followed closely by a fire truck, and the commotion draws Jake from the kitchen. I'm grateful the siren is not on, but when a stretcher is rolled through my front door, it makes such a racket that Jake scrambles up on the step behind me. He reaches out to touch Enid's hair just as the paramedics lift her from my arms and strap her in.

"Are you coming with us?" one of the paramedics asks me, as if there is some scenario in which I'd let them take her away while I just sit and watch.

I motion toward Jacob. "We both are."

He is about to protest when a small, bathrobe-clad figure appears behind him on my front porch. "Audrey, is everything all right?"

Mrs. Speight looks frail, and her eyes are rimmed in red. "No," I tell her. "Enid needs to go to the hospital."

"Oh my," she says, pulling her robe tight. "Would you like me to stay here with Jacob?"

I think about the meltdown that's inevitable the minute Jacob enters the hospital, the familiar awful sounds and smells a reminder of his time there, and I know I can't take him with me. I weigh this with the fallout of leaving Jacob alone with this little old woman who's already wary of him.

"That's good of you to offer, but I don't know if you can really handle . . ."

She moves out of the way as the medics carry Enid out of the house and then steps closer. "Jacob and I will be fine," she says firmly. It looks like she's been crying, too. I should ask if she's okay, but I don't have time. Enid is being loaded into the ambulance.

"Are you sure?"

"Yes, dear. You go on. I can stay all night if you need me." She moves next to Jacob and reaches out a hand. "Do you like macaroni and cheese?" she asks. He smiles shyly, and while he does not take her hand in return, he accepts her invitation and follows her as she makes her way toward the kitchen.

I follow them to grab my purse and keys and take a moment to kiss Jake on the top of his head. He smells just like he does every day, and I know that fifty years from now, I will remember the smell of my little boy. "I love you," I say for the second time today, bending my knees to try to see his face. He closes his eyes so he doesn't have to look at me, but he smiles, unconcerned, and when he does, he looks like just a normal kid. Jake may be anything but normal, but I wonder if the things I think separate him from other kids simply just set him apart.

I run for the ambulance, inwardly pleading with God to make Enid better, to make me better, and to make what happened tonight my final mistake.

CHAPTER TWENTY-ONE

"Did she take anything with the alcohol?" a paramedic asks as I climb into the ambulance. The door closes behind me with a metallic slam, and I wince.

I think for a moment before remembering it was Jake who had a snack this afternoon and not Enid. I left without thinking of the kids, prioritizing myself over them as I have done repeatedly for years. I drink to make myself feel better, but every time I drink, I do it at their expense. I've spent more than half my years as a parent impaired.

"Ma'am?" he asks.

"No," I tell him, "and I don't know if she had lunch today."

"Drugs or medication? Did she take any with the alcohol that you know of?" He says it impatiently, as if I'm supposed to know that's what he meant the first time. I'm sure he has already passed judgment on me, and I can't blame him.

"No, I didn't see anything. But I also didn't think to look." I rack my brain trying to remember if there was anything else lying around Enid's room.

"Is there any chance this was a suicide attempt?"

The question catches me off guard, and I glare at him. He looks at me out of the corner of his eye while he pokes an IV into the back of Enid's hand and tapes it into place.

"*No*," I answer adamantly, though the bruises might be telling another story, one I haven't listened to. I have ignored the signs that my child is not well, and she has had to find another way to get through to me.

"I'm sorry," he says. "I have to ask. It's important that we know what else could be in her system. She looks pretty beat up to me."

"She did that to herself. Right now, I'm pretty sure it's about the alcohol. She was trying to prove a point to me."

"What kind of point?"

"How miserable it is to live with a person who drinks."

He makes a sound that's half laugh, half snort. "Well, she's right about that. My dad was a drunk. It was no fun at all."

A drunk. Though he is referring to his father, I feel like it's the second time today I've been labeled, and it stings.

I sit in silence and watch the lines on a little screen broadcast Enid's vital signs. The stretcher holds her in a sitting position so that if she vomits, she does not choke on it or aspirate it into her lungs. Her face has turned pale, and her lips are a sickly grayish color. I cry silently as the paramedics discuss her slowing respiratory rate, the result of her attempt to show me what it's like to live with me.

My payback for being selfish over and over again is watching while they put a breathing tube down my daughter's throat. My head throbs, and the sounds around me merge to become a constant roar.

At the hospital, Enid is whisked away while I'm forced to sit and fill out paperwork. It's freezing inside the building, and I wrap my arms around myself for warmth. At some point it dawns on me that I should call Stewart, but I push the thought from my mind, deciding to wait because I don't even know what her condition is. I can't call him thousands of miles away and tell him I don't know what's going to happen, and I'm scared of how he will react when he finds out another one of our children has been hospitalized because of me.

"Mrs. Anderson, would you like some coffee?" A small woman wearing a lime-green cardigan appears beside me, holding out a paper cup. Steam rises from the cup and it smells wonderful, but I shake my head, denying myself anything that might bring me comfort.

"My name is Monica, and I'm a social worker here at the hospital. Would you like to come have a seat in my office? It's much warmer in there." She is completely nonthreatening except for the fact that she is a social worker.

"I need to find out where they've taken Enid," I say, looking past her and down the hall in the direction I last saw my daughter.

"She's in good hands, and those good hands are working very hard to make her better right now." She waits for me to look at her before she speaks again. "I really think we should go to my office. I promise not to keep you long, and I'll make sure everyone knows where to find you if there's an update on your daughter."

I sigh, understanding I probably don't have a choice, and follow her to an elevator. There are three other people in the elevator, and every one of them looks miserable. No one comes to a children's hospital for a *good* reason. A child they love is here, sick or hurt, and it's hard to be cheerful when a child is sick or hurt. I have, in a very short period of time, created situations that have landed both of my children here. It's no wonder I'm on my way to talk to a social worker.

We get off the elevator and walk down an empty corridor to the sound of Monica's ballet flats tapping on the floor and echoing off the cinderblock walls. She opens a door for me, and I follow her into a small room furnished with a desk and three armchairs.

"I'm going to stop," I say before she has a chance to sit and accuse me of anything.

She slides the cup of coffee toward me, a second chance. "What are you going to stop?"

"Drinking. This is my fault. She wanted me to know how it feels. That's why she did what she did tonight."

She lowers herself into a chair and folds her hands on top of her desk. "Are you telling me you have a problem with alcohol?"

"Yes."

"Have you sought treatment?"

"No. It hasn't been a problem until now."

"Perhaps it's been a problem for Enid for longer than you realize. We were concerned that Enid might be the one with a problem. That's why I wanted to talk to you."

"She doesn't have a problem other than having a terrible mother," I say. "Well, that's not true, but I suppose right now I'm her biggest problem."

"Well, then, it's good that you're admitting you need help."

"I just needed a wake-up call," I say. "I'm going to stop."

"I think you may find you'll need some help stopping. It's not as easy as just deciding, Mrs. Anderson. You have an addiction."

I wave my arms in front of me. "*This* is the help I need. Both of my kids have been here in the past few weeks because of *me*. It stopped being a problem today."

Monica pulls a legal pad across her desk and picks up a pen. She taps the pen a few times before scribbling a curlicue on the corner of the paper.

"Can you tell me about your other recent visit here?"

Get me out of here. I press my fingertips into my eyelids hard, until I see little pinpricks of light. "I just want to know how my daughter is!"

Without flinching, Monica says, "Then let's get started. The faster we get done here, the sooner you'll see Enid."

Monica has filled two pages of her legal pad with notes and doesn't seem to be running out of questions. I'm fairly honest, but know that if I tell her I was drunk when the accident happened, I will be in serious trouble. *Agitated* doesn't begin to describe how I feel about not knowing anything about how Enid is, but Monica assures me over and over again that the hospital staff knows where I am and that I will be updated as soon as there is something to update me on. The more time that passes, the more I worry that something horrible is happening to her.

I stare at the still untouched coffee cup, suddenly feeling very thirsty. "Can I have some water?" I ask Monica.

"Is tap water okay? There's a staff break room next door with a sink." Monica stands up and heads for the door, and I jump up from my chair.

"Can I come with you? I need to stretch my legs."

"Sure," she shrugs. I follow her from the office and through another door with a narrow window into a small kitchen. A refrigerator hums quietly in the corner, and a microwave sits on the counter. The room smells like tomato soup, and I wonder if someone was in here eating lunch while I was being interrogated by a social worker.

I walk to the sink and turn on the tap, wasting time by sticking my finger under the stream of water waiting for it to run cold. I pull a paper cup from a dispenser next to the sink, fill it, and chug it down. I fill the cup again and drink, my thirst worsening with every swallow.

"Are you okay, Audrey?" It's the first time she's called me by my first name.

"Fine," I say, my back still to her. "Just a little parched."

"Do you think it could be because you aren't drinking what you'd like to be drinking?"

"What are you now, a psychologist?" I say a little too defensively.

"Actually, yes," she says, sounding bolder to match my own tone. "My bachelor's degree was in psychology, and I have master's degrees in both psychology and social work. Most of what I do requires me to use the psychology training."

I want to tell her that I have a master's degree, too, an Ivy League MBA at that, but it almost seems like it's irrelevant now because I'm not that person anymore. I drink more water and she is quiet, but I can't waste time forever. "I'd like to see Enid now. We can talk more later."

I hear a chair move across the floor as she sits down at a small round table. "Enid is being treated for an alcohol overdose. She's fourteen years old. I think what Enid needs most is for you to get *yourself* together. I can help you do that."

I crush the cup in my hand and turn around, leaning against the sink. I'm still thirsty.

"I can get it together," I say.

"Audrey, were either of your parents drinkers?"

I think about what Jane said last week. "They died when I was four," I tell her, squeezing the cup into the smallest ball I can. "I don't really remember them except for a few things."

"How did they die?"

"A car accident."

She raises her eyebrows. "Do you know the cause of the accident?"

"They hit a tree," I snap. "It was nighttime and raining, just like my own accident. Why? Are you going to suggest that my father was an alcoholic like my sister did?"

"I think it's interesting that your sister thinks that, but I'm not trying to suggest anything, Audrey. I'm just exploring, trying to gather information. You and I actually have a lot in common. I lost my parents at a young age, also."

"Oh, really? Was your father a drunk, too? Everyone conveniently has an alcoholic parent today," I snarl, remembering the paramedic's remarks.

"No," she says quietly. "My mother was. She passed out at the kitchen table one night while our dinner was cooking on the stove. A fire started, and she never woke up. Our house burned to the ground." She pauses, waiting for me to say something rude or sarcastic. I don't.

"She died in the fire. I was able to get two of my siblings out, but my youngest brother hid under a bed because he was scared, and by the time the firemen found him, he was gone. He was five."

"How old were you?"

"Eleven." Just like Jane. Jane remembers our father drinking. I don't.

"I'm sorry," I say.

"A social worker was put in charge of our case and was the best person I'd ever met. Still is to this day. He cared about us so much and made sure the three of us stayed together in foster care. He's the reason I became a social worker."

"What about your father?" I ask, thinking about Stewart.

"He committed suicide when I was eight."

I let this sink in. No wonder her mother was an alcoholic—four kids and a husband who killed himself.

"I know what you're thinking," Monica says, "and you're wrong."

"What am I thinking?"

"That she had every right to drink. That a dead husband and a bunch of kids would drive anyone to drink." I look down at my feet, embarrassed that she's right.

"The thing is, that's exactly why she had *no right* to do it. We depended on her for everything. Food, clothing, shelter, safety . . . love would have been icing on the cake. She was our mother *and* our father, and she let us down time after time. Not only that, but she passed on a predisposition to addiction, Audrey. Did you know that children of alcoholics are between three and eight times more likely to become addicts themselves?"

"Actually, I do know that. Why, are you an alcoholic?"

"No, but only because I've never taken a drink. I *do* have an addictive personality, though, and I know what could happen."

"So what are you addicted to?" I think of Debbie Abbott. If Monica tells me she's addicted to shopping, I'm walking out of here.

"Exercise."

I laugh, because it sounds almost as ridiculous as shopping. "Well, good for you. I bet you're in terrific shape." No wonder she's so tiny.

"Yes and no," she says. "In order to satisfy the compulsion, I run between six and twelve miles a day, six days a week. I have almost no body fat, which might seem like a good thing except that my husband and I have tried unsuccessfully for six years to have a baby. My body is just too screwed up."

I read somewhere once that the same thing happens to female gymnasts. "Can't you just run less?"

She smiles, but beneath it there is an unmistakable sadness. "I've tried, but running is my addiction. The farther I run, the better I feel. If I didn't run, I'd find some other, unhealthier replacement for it, so we decided—my husband and I—to let it be what it is."

I stand there and think about what she's been saying, that alcoholism can be genetic. I don't know if my father's drinking caused the accident that killed him and my mother, but my sister obviously seems to think it's possible and that the addiction gene has been passed on to me. I think about Enid's obsession with carbohydrates and fat, and the bruises, and I wonder if those could be the start of some kind of addiction, or compulsion at the very least.

She folds her hands on the table, going back to her set position. "Look. You did not lose your son in the car accident, but you could have. I don't believe you are going to lose Enid today, but you could have. What is it going to take to make you see how close you have come to losing everything, or worse yet, leaving *them* with nothing? They probably already have a predisposition to addiction, though fortunately Jacob is an unlikely candidate for drug or alcohol use, but what about Enid? She's been through a lot lately and might be looking for a crutch. *You* must be her crutch, Audrey. Teach her better ways to cope."

"You're right . . . about all of it," I say. "This is all I need to hear. I'm done. I mean it."

"And I'm telling you that it's not enough to decide to quit. You need treatment. A program to help you make sure that one addiction doesn't become another." I think again of Debbie and her pills. Of the pills I've been taking myself.

"Please let me see my daughter," I say, suddenly more tired than I have ever been in my life. "Just let me see with my own eyes that she's okay, and then I promise we can talk more."

Monica stands and pushes the door open, holding it for me. I follow, feeling ashamed and alone, but not thirsty anymore.

CHAPTER TWENTY-TWO

Enid is sleeping, but her color is better, and the doctors have removed the breathing tube. I've been watching her for hours, thinking about what I will say to her when she wakes up.

A nurse comes in to do whatever it is she seems to be required to do on a very regular basis. I tell her I'm going outside to use my phone and to please come get me if Enid wakes up. She assures me she will, and as I leave the room, I hear her talking sweetly to my unconscious daughter, as if Enid can hear her. I feel a sharp pang of regret that I didn't appreciate all that my nurse, Tina, did for me when I was in the hospital. Nurses are the most underappreciated people on Earth,

I think—nurses and special education teachers. Maybe guidance counselors, too.

When I get outside the hospital lobby and finally have a signal, there are a dozen missed calls and voice mails from Stewart. He's freaking out because he called the house and "the old lady from next door" answered, telling him I'd left with Enid in an ambulance. I certainly can't blame him.

"What the hell happened this time?" he asks on the first ring when I finally work up the nerve to dial his number. "And why do I have to hear it from a total stranger who's sitting in our house watching my son?"

I immediately go on the defensive. "Look, you don't even remember Mrs. Speight's name, and we've lived next door to her for seven years. Don't get all self-righteous when you're thousands of miles away."

Stewart sighs. "Sometimes I think you forget that they're my kids, too. I may not be there, but I am very concerned for their well-being."

"Sometimes I think *you* forget they're your kids, Stewart, but it's great to know you're concerned about their well-being. What about mine, huh?"

"Pardon me? You're a grown woman, Audrey. You are responsible for your own well-being. *We* are responsible for the kids'." He sounds angrier than I can ever remember him being. Stewart is a conflict avoider. Usually when we argue he shuts down, leaves town, and works. Now that he's ready to fight, so am I.

"You've left me for years in a situation where I'm solely and completely responsible, and I can't handle it. You know I can't handle it, and you know how I deal with it. How does that benefit the kids' well-being?" A couple of people walk past me toward the hospital entrance, but I make no effort to lower my voice. If I'm going to own up to my problems, the entire world might as well know about them.

"Audrey, stop. Can you please at least fill me in on what's happened before you berate me for being a terrible husband and father? Why is Enid in the hospital?"

It's pitch-dark outside, and a chilly, damp breeze tickles my neck. I have no idea what time it is. I spot a bench along the sidewalk under a streetlamp and sit down on it.

"You're going to blame me for this," I begin, pulling my left arm tightly around me, "and you're not wrong to, but you have to know that I never meant for anything like this to happen, for the kids to get hurt." I tell him everything. I tell him how far back this goes and how deep. How much I've resented him and the kids and how often I've wished Jacob was not . . . Jacob, but that I don't feel that way anymore.

I expect tears to come, but they don't. I'm so grateful that Enid is okay, that Jake is okay, and that I didn't get one of my children killed because of my own selfishness that I don't feel sad anymore. I'm angry, regretful, and disgusted with myself, and I know there's a chance I won't get away with it this time, but I have to accept it and face it. Enid did what she did because I was not paying attention to her cries for help, and when she wakes up in that hospital bed, she may never be able to trust or forgive me.

I tell Stewart about Monica, too. "You have to come home immediately so they don't take the kids away. I will do whatever I have to do to fix things and be a good mother. I don't know if I've *ever* been one, but I can. I will, I promise."

"I'm in a taxi, Audrey, on my way to the airport. I don't know how much help I can be—my track record speaks for itself—but I promise I'll try. We both have some things we need to fix, not just you."

The sky is beginning to lighten in the distance as I hang up and wander back into the hospital. When I reach Enid's floor, a familiar face greets me with a smile. "I was just going to send someone to look for you," the nurse says cheerfully. "Your girl is up."

I let out a loud *whoop* and can't get to her room fast enough, even though I still haven't decided what I'm going to say to her. The nurse catches up to me and places a gentle hand on my shoulder. "She's feeling a little rough, so go easy on her . . . at least for now."

I like that she is thinking of Enid's best interest and know it's something I need to do better, so we continue down the hall together. Enid looks up from her bed as we enter the room, and her lips tighten into a forced smile. "Hi, Mom."

"Hi, E." It's such a physical relief to see her awake that I know I'll do whatever I have to from this point forward to fix the mess I made.

She tries to prop herself up on her elbows, but she's so weak. The nurse hurries to adjust the back of her bed to a sitting position before leaving us alone.

"I'm sorry," she says when the room is quiet, giant tears beginning the journey down the hollows of her cheeks. It wasn't long ago that she was innocent and unscathed, but here she is, just fourteen years old, recovering from an alcohol overdose while a naked photo of her floats around cyberspace. I'd ask myself how we got here if I didn't already know the answer.

"Please don't apologize to me," I say. "This is my fault. All of it." I sit on the edge of her bed and grab hold of her tiny, cold hands.

"I didn't mean to make you mad by telling Mrs. Franklin about you. I just didn't know who else to talk to about it."

I reach up and wipe her tears away. "You did the right thing by telling her. If you had talked to your dad, he probably would have brushed it off, and I hate to admit it, but I'd probably have lied to you. I was definitely lying to myself. I think Dad and I were both in denial about how serious this was."

"Were?"

"Yes, I recognize now that I have a problem, and I ignored it even after it got your brother hurt. The fact that you felt you had to hurt yourself to get my attention means that you were far more angry and afraid than you could handle." Enid lets out a big breath, like a balloon deflating. "I'm so embarrassed about the kind of mother I've been when you needed me the most."

"What about Dad?"

"I just talked to him. He's on his way home. I've talked with a social worker, too. Her name is Monica, and I have a feeling you'll meet her soon. She's going to help me find a treatment program and will find a family counselor to help us get through all this together."

"A treatment program? Are you going to have to go away?" She looks sad, like it would be a bad thing if I had to go away, and this is comforting.

"I honestly don't know, but I hope not," I say. "I'd like to work on being a better parent at the same time I'm working on being a sober person. I think they kind of go together."

"So . . ." she says, squirming uncomfortably, "*are* you an alcoholic?"

"Yes," I say, and she looks both surprised and relieved.

"Cool," she says and quickly backtracks. "Not cool that you're an alcoholic, but cool that you're, like, aware of it." She bites her lip. "Does that make sense?"

"It does," I say, and maybe it's just a fleeting feeling, but right now a lot of things make sense that haven't in a very long time. We sit in a comfortable silence for a while, and I keep my hand on hers, feeling the warmth return to it.

"Mom?" she says after a long time.

"Yes?"

"Can we just be even now?" Her eyes are teary again, and I recognize in them extreme regret.

"Oh, Enid. I would love to say yes, but I've got a lot I need to do before I will catch up and be even with you again. I'm going to get there, though. I promise." Her face relaxes, as if I've just lifted the weight of the world off her shoulders.

"I look forward to that," she says as she closes her eyes and drifts off, her face calm and serene despite the events of the past few hours.

I feel a surge of pride and affection toward Enid that I haven't felt in a long time, and I want her to feel the same for me one day. I want her to be able to be proud that I am her mother and to know in the deepest recesses of her heart that I am there for her. I pull Monica's card from my purse and step out of the room to call her, stopping first to kiss my sleeping daughter on her head and whisper to her that I love her.

CHAPTER TWENTY-THREE

As I turn into my driveway, I stop for a minute before pulling into the garage. I look at my beautiful house. Everything is pristine on the outside—the grass is neatly trimmed, flowers spill out of pots on my front porch, and there is not a thing out of place. Who would guess that there has been so much turmoil inside this perfect house?

Sighing, I maneuver my car into the garage and turn off the engine. I enter the kitchen to find Mrs. Speight sitting at the table with a stack of Jacob's books and a cup of hot tea. She's been here with Jacob for nearly eighteen hours, but I checked in with her late last night, and she said Jacob was in bed fast asleep and that she was making herself comfortable in the guest room across the hall. She certainly looks no worse for the wear today.

"Just by the look on your face, I can tell that Enid is doing better," Mrs. Speight says as I set down my purse and keys. "Can I get you some tea, dear?"

I guess at some point I'm going to have to learn to drink new things, so I accept her offer. She shuffles to the stove and turns the flame on under a kettle I forgot I even had. While she busies herself in my kitchen, I peek through the doorway to find Jacob in his usual place in the living room, but the television isn't on. He has a clipboard in his lap and a box of crayons on the sofa beside him. He never colors. In fact, the last time he did, he got so frustrated he broke half the crayons in the box and threw the rest across the room. I crawled around picking up the salvageable ones and put them back in the box, long forgotten until Mrs. Speight unearthed them from whatever tomb they've been in since then.

I move closer to look at Jacob's "picture." It's abstract and beautiful, swaths of color covering the page in random shapes almost like stained glass. He presses hard on the paper, and the tip of the orange crayon in his hand snaps off. I hold my breath, waiting for the hysteria I know will follow, but he picks up the yellow and green box, turns it around, and pushes the broken crayon into the sharpener on the back with such skill and patience that I almost can't believe I'm watching my own son.

A small, fragile hand touches my shoulder, and I turn to see Mrs. Speight holding out a steaming mug of tea. "I took the liberty of adding sugar, Audrey. I hope you don't mind my saying so, but you look like you could use the calories."

I cannot imagine what I look like. I can't remember the last time I ate and must look positively haggard after a night in the hospital with Enid. I thank Mrs. Speight and sip the tea. It's sweet and strong and soothes me as the warmth runs down my throat. It's a different kind of warmth than alcohol, but I just may be able to get used to it.

"I can't believe Jacob is coloring," I say, looking back into the next room as Jake pulls a light green crayon from the box.

"He seemed a little agitated when he woke up. I'm sure it was because you and Enid weren't here, and the strange old lady from next door still was." Mrs. Speight smiles. "I made some breakfast but he didn't want any, so I went looking and found the crayons and coloring books in a drawer. The lines in the coloring book upset him—he kept trying to wipe them away—so we went to my house for some plain paper and the clipboard, and he's been peaceful ever since. My children loved to draw and color when they were his age." She sips from her own cup of tea and adds, "He's welcome to keep the clipboard."

"Thank you," I say, though those two words fail to properly recognize the gratitude I feel about what I'm seeing. Mrs. Speight is right. Jake is *peaceful* right now, in a way he hasn't been since Bud has been gone. Memories of the time before I screwed my family up come flooding back, and I have to blink away tears.

"I hope Jacob was sweet to Reuben while he was at your house," I say, wondering if his obsession with the dog next door will be renewed after going to Mrs. Speight's today.

She looks down at her cup, and sadness washes over her, deepening the lines on her face, making her age right before my eyes. It's how she looked last night when the ambulance was here.

"I had to put Reuben down the day before yesterday," she says, her voice uneven.

"What?" I gasp. "I'm so sorry to hear that." I can't think of anything else to say. Her pain is so visible, and no words I can possibly come up with will make it better.

"He was having trouble walking, and the veterinarian found a cancerous mass in his hip. It spread very quickly. I barely had time to adjust to the news before I had to make the decision to put him to sleep. There was nothing they could do, and he was suffering so badly." She begins to cry, so I lead her back to the kitchen table and pull out a chair.

"You never knew Howard, my husband, but when he passed away, I thought I would never be happy again. I really don't remember the first two years after he died.

My children came to check on me but never stayed long. You know how people are, so busy with jobs and families . . . life goes on . . . but I was so alone. At one point I completely stopped eating. I think I was somehow trying to die along with Howard.

"I spoke with my doctor about how sad I was feeling, and he gave me some pills he said would help. Well, they may as well have been magic beans. I knew nothing I could wash down with a glass of water was going to make me feel any better."

I think about the antidepressants I'd been taking myself and understand what she means.

"So one day I went to the bookshop on Maple to look for books on coping with the death of a spouse. There used to be a little pet store next door to it, and that day when I walked past, I happened to look in the window. Reuben was in a playpen with some other puppies, and he looked right at me. His little brown eyes reminded me of Howard's little brown eyes—some people might have called them beady, but to me they were the kindest eyes I've ever seen. I forgot all about that book, went inside, and picked Reuben up out of that pen. I truly believe he was meant for me, and when I brought him home, I felt love again. I felt *loved* again. I had a purpose, someone to take care of.

"I know Reuben wasn't a some*one*, but to me he was. I had to start taking care of myself again so I wouldn't let him down. Now that he's gone, I feel lost all over again. My house is so empty and quiet, so I've enjoyed being here with Jacob, with another someone."

I search for something to say, but I still can't come up with anything besides *I'm sorry*, so Mrs. Speight's beautiful words hang in the air, undisturbed. Her sadness found happiness and then became sadness again, but Jacob has brought her happiness for now, for today. I have failed to allow Jacob to bring me joy and peace simply by virtue of him being *my* someone, and I have failed to nurture Enid because I haven't nurtured myself. I've turned every complicated situation into a problem that can only be solved with a drink, and it nearly cost me everything . . . twice.

"And I'm sorry," Mrs. Speight says, surprising me, because I can't think of a thing she should be apologizing for.

"You're sorry for what?"

"I'm sorry I stopped letting Jacob come see Reuben. I was a terrible neighbor. I just didn't understand . . ."

"I didn't, either," I interrupt. "You were no worse a neighbor than I was a mother. I'm still trying to figure Jacob out, and in just one day, you've done a better job understanding what he needs than I have in a long time."

She reaches out and pats my hand. Her hand is soft and warm from holding her tea, and the touch is comforting. "I wish I could say or do something to make you feel better," I tell her.

"Maybe we can be better friends. In the true sense of being neighbors, maybe we can spend more time together. I'd like to help you again if you ever need it." She keeps patting my hand in rhythm with her sentiments.

"But that's you helping me. What can I do for you?"

"Just spend time with a lonely, forgotten, old woman. I don't know if at my age I should get another dog, and I wonder if I'd ever love another one as much as I did Reuben. I think I was lucky to have one true love of my life that was human and one that was an animal. I'm afraid everyone else will come up a little short." Her eyes shine with fond memories of her loves.

"Where's that beast of yours, by the way?" she asks. "I haven't seen a trace of fur or even a dog dish, and something told me mentioning it to Jacob might not be a good idea."

"We lost Bud, too," I say, and without planning to, it all comes out in a flood of release as I finally own up to all I've done to hurt my family—not just in the last few months, but for years without even being aware of it.

Mrs. Speight is a wonderful listener. My confession clearly surprises her, but she is not about to let me off the hook. Like Monica, she asks me what I'm going to do about my problem now that I can admit I have one, and she tells me she will support me in any way she can. She tells me I have a responsibility to my kids that nobody else does, not even Stewart.

"I don't believe in guardian angels," she says, "because the work of guardian angels is done here on Earth every single day by mothers. They serve and protect their children and families like no heavenly being ever could. You've lost your way, Audrey, but now your path is clearly lit. It's your choice to follow it."

All I can do is nod and smile at this wise woman through rapidly falling tears.

"So let's make a plan." Mrs. Speight straightens up in her chair, very businesslike now that my emotions have been set free.

Jacob appears in the doorway, coloring paper in hand. He looks surprised to see the two of us sitting there but doesn't seem to notice that I've been crying. He smiles his crooked smile after a moment and hands the paper to Mrs. Speight.

"That's lovely," she tells him. "So many beautiful colors! I bet your mom would like to see it, too." She places her hands gently on his shoulders and turns him toward me. I reach out for the paper, but Jacob clutches it to his chest and crawls into my lap instead.

I wrap my arms around my son, wanting to hold him as tight as I can for all the times I have failed to hold him at all. I also want him to stay in my arms for as long as he will tolerate it, so I give him another gentle squeeze and ask to see his drawing. It's obvious he has put immeasurable thought and care into this work of art, and the pride on his face brings me to tears again.

"Let's put this in a frame on the wall, Jake. I want to be able to look at it every day."

Jacob scampers from my lap and back into the living room, but I can still feel the weight of him in my lap and smell his little boy smell. It's these kinds of things I have completely taken for granted, but I promise myself I won't anymore. Jacob may be an autistic child who frustrates me and creates situations that make me unsure and uncomfortable, but I know now that he is so much more than that. He is a child—*my child*—who will surprise me with his specialness if I take the time to really pay attention. He is my future and I am his, and I finally see that our future together will be greater than I was ever able to imagine.

I suddenly remember why I came home and jump up from the table. "I forgot! I have to get some clothes for Enid and go back to the hospital," I say. "I think she'll be able to come home tomorrow."

Mrs. Speight stays seated at the table and nods. "I have nowhere to go and nothing to do, so I'll be happy to stay here with Jacob."

I don't want her to think I assumed she'd stay even though I didn't ask. "I can take him with me if you'd like to go home and have some peace. You've gone above and beyond already."

"Don't be silly. Hospitals are no place for healthy children." She stands and picks up the teacups. "Go back to Enid. Bring her home. Then start fresh."

I hug her, rattling the cups in her hands, and feel her tiny shoulders, bony and fragile in my embrace. "I'm so grateful for you," I say and then stop short. "Has Jacob had any accidents? I forgot to warn you that sometimes he does."

"No, dear," she says. "He's been a perfect gentleman."

She shoos me out of the kitchen, but I hear her at the sink as I head upstairs, rinsing dishes and humming. If Mrs. Speight finds joy and purpose in helping a mess like me, I'll be happy to have her.

I throw Enid's favorite sweats and a pair of fuzzy socks into a bag and look around. Her room is exactly as it was when I called the ambulance yesterday. I yank aside her curtains and open the window to let some fresh air in, then start stripping her bedsheets.

I remake the bed with clean linens and roll the vodka bottle up in the old sheets to dispose of when I get downstairs. I see her phone perched on the edge of her desk and notice the glass on the screen is cracked. I haven't seen Enid using it much lately—and from what she has said, she's been avoiding people since her public embarrassment, even Hannah—but she never mentioned to me that her phone is broken.

Careful not to slice my finger open on the cracked glass, I press the home button and swipe. I haven't checked her Instagram account in weeks. My mind has been in such a fog, it hasn't occurred to me to do it, and in truth, part of me knew what I'd see there.

When I press the icon and go to her posts page, I'm relieved to see there aren't any new ones, but I'm not prepared at all for what I see on her activity page. There are comments—dozens of them—directed at @enid521, crucifying her for the photo and the unremarkable nature of her fourteen-year-old breasts. Surely this is just a fraction of the people who have actually seen the photo, and only the ones who are cruel enough to publicly comment on it. It's positively frightening. There is an inbox for private messages, but I can't bring myself to click on it. I cannot even imagine what I might find there.

I sit on the edge of the bed and cry for my daughter as I read the words she has been abused by alone in this room. She has been dealing with the aftershocks of this situation with absolutely no help from me. It's no wonder she felt compelled to talk to her guidance counselor, since the only thing I gave Enid to go on is how I was dealing with my own problems.

My heartbeat increases as I consider for the first time that perhaps Enid's drinking binge could have been an attempt to make it all go away, to clean her slate, so to speak. Her friends have turned their backs on her, and her family was never really here for her to begin with.

I know what it's like not having my parents to raise me, but without realizing it, I have created a very similar life for my children. Enid has been raising herself, and at times, her brother, though she is not emotionally mature enough to do either.

If I ever needed a reason to stop drinking, this is it. I may not be the mother Enid and Jake deserve, but I'm the only one they've got. Like Enid said, she's stuck with me, and I absolutely cannot let them down again. I finish straightening up Enid's room, tuck her broken cell phone into my back pocket, and pick up the bag I packed for her. I'm going to bring my baby girl home.

CHAPTER TWENTY-FOUR

Every one of us is in dire need of counseling. Not long ago, I'd probably have said that people who need counseling are either too weak or too lazy to solve their own problems, but while I've never felt a stronger desire to make changes in my life, they are simply too monumental for me to tackle on my own.

Monica is right. I cannot stop drinking without help. The process of facing my bad choices and their consequences is so agonizing that it makes me contemplate a drink to numb the pain almost constantly, even though I know what it's cost me and that I could have lost so much more. Being around Stewart makes me want to drink, too. Every conversation we have now turns into an argument, each of us wanting to alleviate our own guilt by blaming the other. He reminds me every chance he gets of my irresponsible actions, and I immediately throw back in his face his complete and total inaction. While I know that what I have done is far worse—putting both of my children in harm's way repeatedly—he seems to think he's just an innocent bystander, rather than a distant father with a blindfold on to what's been happening to his family.

I am halfway through a two-week-long outpatient rehabilitation program, so Stewart has had to stay home with Jacob, who is still not back at school, and Enid, who has been given permission to finish the semester online. Mrs. Speight offered to come help out from eight to three while I'm gone, but when I relayed this to Stewart, he angrily stated that he is "perfectly capable of taking care of his own children and seeing that they return to school as soon as humanly possible."

Today I am greeted at the door by yelling. I hear Stewart's voice at full volume, followed by Enid's. The sounds are coming from upstairs, but I set down my things, hesitant to get involved with whatever is happening. I check the living room for Jacob, but the television is not on, and there is no sign of him. The kitchen is a mess, half-eaten lunches on the table and dishes piled up in the sink. When the yelling starts up again, I reluctantly head upstairs in the event a referee is needed.

Enid's room is quiet, but her bedspread is covered in schoolbooks, and her new laptop, complete with filters that block all social media, sits open on her bedside table. I continue down the hall toward the noise, and it's just as I enter Jacob's room that I realize the shouts emanating from there are not angry shouts, but encouraging ones.

"That's a heck of a nugget, Jake!" Stewart hollers.

"Great poop, Jakey!" Enid chirps.

The toilet flushes, and my family emerges from the bathroom, triumphant.

"Hi, Mom," Enid says when she sees me. "Jake just pooped on the potty, didn't you, buddy?" She holds her hand up, and Jake high-fives it, with his palm, not the back of his hand.

Stewart is beaming. "I'm not sure who worked the hardest in there," he says. "Cheerleading is exhausting."

Jacob looks proud as I kneel in front of him. "You went poop on the potty? Good boy!" I look up at Stewart. "You know, we should get some Skittles as incentive, like we did when he was little."

Stewart reaches into his jeans pocket and pulls out a red bag. "Thought of it already," he says, neither defensively nor snidely, though I can't help feeling outdone. I'd have thought that Stewart wouldn't remember such a detail. Maybe Enid suggested it, but I don't ask. I remind myself that regardless of who is responsible for making it happen, Jake is making progress again, and that's what matters. I tousle his hair, and he runs from the room.

Enid excuses herself to get back to her schoolwork, and Stewart and I follow Jacob downstairs, where he has knelt at the coffee table to color. I wonder if he's watched much TV today, but I don't ask because I don't want to know if Stewart has done better at engaging with Jake, too.

We sit down in the kitchen, and Stewart starts fiddling with a coffeepot I've never seen before. "Want some coffee?" he asks.

"No, thanks. When did we get that?" Neither of us have ever been coffee drinkers except for an occasional Starbucks.

"I went out and picked it up this morning. I've gotten really into coffee since being in Tokyo, and I actually started having withdrawal." He doesn't seem to realize what he's just said. "This isn't going to be nearly as good as what I'm used to, but it'll do," he says, scooping grounds out of an expensive-looking bag and dumping them into the filter.

I'm quiet for a few seconds as he fills the reservoir with water and turns the pot on. "I thought Japan was more of a tea place."

He lets out a chuckle. "Oh, you wouldn't believe the coffee culture that has popped up in recent years. There's a café we stop at every morning on the way to the office that turns out the most beautiful cappuccinos. They really are works of art, and so good."

I imagine Stewart—and someone else, since he said "we"—stepping into a Japanese café to sip on their "works of art." He says it like he just did it this morning, and I realize that to him, *that's* his real life, not the life he's been forced back into here.

"Great job getting Jake to go to the bathroom," I say encouragingly. "You've done better than I have." I want Stewart to feel needed here, like this is where he should be.

He gestures at the bag of Skittles on the counter. "I'd give the candy the credit."

"Still, it's progress." Stewart only shrugs at this, unwilling to take the compliment. It irks me. The coffeepot beeps, indicating the coffee is ready.

"You sure you don't want any?" he asks.

"I'm sure. They want us to try to drink just water for a while." *They* are my counselors at rehab, but I don't want to say it. "Apparently a caffeine addiction can often follow . . . you know . . . so I'm just going to drink water. Thanks, though."

"Wow," he says, taking a loud sip. I don't know whether it's because the coffee is delicious or if he just remembered where I've been all day. An uncomfortable silence follows, and I guess Stewart thinks we're done talking, because he picks up his phone and suddenly it's speaking a foreign language.

"What's that?" I ask.

"Oh," he says. "It's an app I'm using to learn Japanese. It's pretty cool." He pokes at the screen, and it talks some more. He laughs like it's just said something hilarious.

"Can you put it away for a minute?"

Stewart looks annoyed but swipes out of the app and sets the phone facedown on the counter. The island is between us, so I ask him to come sit at the table with me.

"We need to talk."

He looks over my shoulder into the living room. "Jacob's in there," he whispers, as if I'm suggesting we discuss the fact that the tooth fairy isn't real . . . in front of a child who might possibly understand.

"I know. I just want to talk, not argue." My heart starts racing, but when he sits down next to me and takes both of my hands, it gives me courage to ask something I've wanted to ask for a long time. "Do you love me?"

Stewart makes a face. "What kind of question is that?"

"An honest one. I feel like you've left us, like even today you're still living in Tokyo, missing your life there. But I'm hoping I'm wrong and that you see how much we need you here. How much we *want* you around."

Stewart lets go of my hands and rubs his thighs slowly, thinking about what he's going to say to that. "Audrey," he says finally, "you and the kids are very important to me, you know that."

"That's not what I asked," I say.

"Let me finish. You're so important to me, and everything I've done, I've done with the three of you in mind . . ."

"But there are *four* of us."

"Damn it, Audrey!" he snaps. "I told you to let me finish!" He lowers his voice. "Please, just let me finish." He rubs his forehead like his head hurts, and I wait for him to organize his thoughts. I asked him a question he has still not answered, but I force myself to be quiet and not point this out until he's done figuring out what to say to me.

"It's no secret that I feel helpless around the kids. The potty victory today aside, every interaction between the kids and me feels artificial somehow. I don't feel connected to them, and I don't think they feel connected to me. I'm just not a nurturing person, Audrey. It bothers me, feels like an inconvenience, and before you interrupt me again and accuse me of calling our kids an inconvenience, I'm going to be really honest and say you're right. My concern for you, Enid, and Jacob is very real. When I heard about the accident, I couldn't get on a plane fast enough, and when you told me about Enid, I promised myself I would come home and help fix everything." He pauses, and I'm shocked to see real tears in his eyes for the first time ever.

"When I'm here, though, I'm just reminded how disconnected I am. I feel like an actor pretending to be a father, and not even a particularly good one at that. I care about all of you, and I really did take this job in your best interest, because if I didn't, I'd be here hating it and resenting my family. You don't deserve that."

The tears in my eyes have surpassed his and fall freely down my cheeks. I bite my lower lip to keep from interjecting again and saying something hurtful. It's time for me to stop doing that.

"When I'm working, especially on this project, I feel like a whole person, like I'm doing the right thing for me by working on something I'm really passionate about and *good at*. I'm supporting you and the kids comfortably—financially, at least—and that's the best I can do. To answer your question is hard because I do love you. I just don't love being with you, and I start to hate myself the more I realize it."

His tears are falling as quickly as mine now, and my chest hurts. I gasp for air, wondering for a moment if I am having a heart attack, but I know deep down that Stewart has just broken my heart for the final time.

He may only feel whole when he's away, but I know the only thing that will make me whole again is to take care of Enid and Jacob. They are all I have left.

CHAPTER TWENTY-FIVE

Sometimes I still think I want a drink. I get this crazy, fleeting idea that I can literally wash away sadness and disappointment, but now it only lasts a second or two until reality and sense come running to the rescue before I can act on it. My therapist warned me that this is a part of the process, that even though most of the time I'm pleased and proud that I've quit drinking, I will still occasionally feel like I've lost a part of myself I'd gotten very comfortable with.

The thing—or things, rather—that keep me from going backward are Enid and Jacob. I can't look at either of them without thinking about what my life would be like had my actions taken them from me. I dream about the accident, but in my dreams, Jacob doesn't make it. I dream that Enid, too, dies in the ambulance before it reaches the hospital. I wake from the dreams, sweating and shaking, knowing that the guilt and despair—the weight of my responsibility—would have killed me, too.

In the daylight, however, as we learn to live in a new way and I learn to be the best I can be without help from a bottle, I find new things every day to be grateful for. The things that used to make me want to drink now serve as reminders of how messy and colorful life is meant to be.

Enid has forgiven me, but she has yet to forgive herself. Between the naked photo, the self-harm, and the overdose, she has a lot on her plate to work through, and everyone says it will take time. She has started seeing a fantastic child psychologist twice a week and has been paired up with two young women who have been through similar experiences, so hopefully she will be able to see that she'll eventually come out on the other side of all this and live a normal life again.

Stewart leans against the kitchen counter and watches as Mrs. Speight makes homemade chicken and dumplings. Enid and Jacob sit at the table working on an art project together, Enid cutting colored paper into geometric shapes so that Jake can glue each shape onto plain, white paper in mosaic form.

I look at my busy, productive kitchen and wish I could stay and take part in what's going on, but I have somewhere to be. I walk in and set my purse on the table, careful not to disturb the artists. Enid looks up and smiles, something she's started doing more often recently.

"You look nice, Mom," she says, prompting Stewart and Mrs. Speight to look up from the doughballs being rolled on the counter.

"You do," Stewart says, sounding surprised. He leans around the island to get a good look. "Is that a new top?"

"No," I say. "It's been in my closet for years. I guess I just forgot I had it." I smooth down the fabric of the flowing, jade-green blouse self-consciously, but the compliments make me feel good.

"Well, it's a lovely color on you," Mrs. Speight says, dropping a dumpling into a pot of boiling broth.

I take a deep breath and hold it while I count to ten.

"Are you nervous?" Enid asks.

"A little," I lie. I've never been more nervous in my life.

She smiles again, this time more reserved, her lips pressed tightly together. "That's probably really normal the first time."

I nod and exhale, letting my breath out slowly and wishing my heart would stop racing.

I kiss both of my children on the tops of their heads, breathing in their scent so I can take it with me. I laugh when Jake reaches up to wipe the kiss out of his hair, and I make Stewart and Mrs. Speight promise to save me a plate of dinner. Mustering up every bit of courage I can, I walk out to my car and start the engine.

━━✦✦━━

There are five people in the room when I arrive. They chat in a familiar way that tells me they know each other, but a middle-aged man wearing a John Deere hat gives me a friendly wave as I walk past. I find a chair on the end of the second row and sit down, my fingers wrapped tightly around the straps of my purse. It feels like the first day of school.

Within a few minutes, many of the chairs are filled, and an attractive older woman with a perfectly cut silver bob and a strand of pearls around her neck stands at the front of the room and speaks.

"Good evening, ladies and gentlemen. This is the regular meeting of the Royal Oaks group of Alcoholics Anonymous. My name is Michelle, and I am an alcoholic and your secretary."

I relax a little, though I can still feel my pulse pounding in my ears. Even though I spent two weeks in rehab, this feels so *public* and intimidating. It's the next logical step for me, but I'm terrified.

Michelle looks as though she is presiding over a corporate board meeting, not an AA meeting. I glance around, trying to get a look at the group now assembled. There are more men than women, but ages seem to range from early thirties to around seventy. One or two look like I'd expect an alcoholic to look, tired and a bit disheveled, but most look like people I'd see at the grocery store or a school PTA function. Just normal people sitting in metal folding chairs listening to another responsible adult speak. They look like me.

When the room begins to recite the Serenity Prayer in unison, I'm caught off guard. Enid looked it up and printed it out for me, but I haven't memorized it yet.

When the prayer ends, Michelle continues speaking, explaining that AA is a fellowship of men and women and is meant to be a safe place to share our experiences, strength, and hope with each other so that we may solve our common problem. *Our common problem.*

I always felt that my drinking was a way to handle my problems as I perceived them. During the meeting, I'm reminded that I have created a new, far more destructive problem, because I did not have the ability to cope with my perceived ones. I am here because I chose to drink.

I feel so overwhelmed that when new members are given the opportunity to introduce themselves, I can't do it. I know that my transgressions are written all over my face, and I'm afraid that if I stand up, I will be turned away for the horrendous things I've done. My drinking was not done in a vacuum where it didn't hurt anyone— it hurt my family in ways I may never understand the full extent of.

I promise myself I will gather the courage to stand up next week. These people are supposed to be a support system for me, something I sorely need. I will get up and be brave, but I just can't do it today.

I think about Enid and Jacob, at home right now eating dinner with Stewart and Mrs. Speight. I'm not there because I am here, which feels like I'm letting them down yet again. So I change my mind and decide the time to be brave is now, and even though the moment has passed for the group, I stand up, and every head in the room turns toward me.

Michelle looks up, surprised at first, but then smiles, her kind eyes creasing in the corners as a dimple forms in her left cheek. It's such a warm, sincere smile that it helps me take the next step.

"I'm sorry. I wasn't sure I was ready," I say. "I'm so nervous." Several people nod, perhaps familiar with how frightening this is. I wipe my damp, shaky palms on my pants and take a deep breath. "I'm Audrey. I'm an alcoholic."

"Hi, Audrey," the group says in unison. Not everyone is smiling like Michelle, but there is compassion on every face. They've already stood where I am, and they are not going to cast me out. I sit down, proud of myself for being braver than I thought, though somewhere in the back of my mind, I know this isn't even close to being the hardest thing I'm going to have to do.

For the rest of the meeting, I listen to people talk about how their decisions to drink have not only threatened to ruin their lives, but also the lives of the people they cared about the most. Marriages have been torn apart, and children have been taken away. Some talk about how their behavior was introduced at a very young age, by watching their own parents, and I think about my parents and the circumstances surrounding their deaths. Was my father drunk behind the wheel? Was he drunk most of the time? Were his selfish choices responsible for leaving Jane and me without parents?

I think about Enid especially and if this will become a pattern in her own life later on. I feel like it's up to me to make sure it doesn't.

When the meeting ends, I am inspired by the courage it takes for the people in this room to show up every week. I have to admit, I also feel a bit discouraged to know how common alcoholism is and how difficult it is to get sober. I've thought about how great a drink would *feel*, not taste, at least four times since I got here, and I wonder how long it will be before I can get through a day without that happening.

There is a table off to the side with coffee and cookies on it, which many of the attendees head over to. My first instinct is to hurry from the room and to my car, but since I have decided to be brave, I stay and take my place behind a few meeting-goers and wait my turn. A man a little older than me, built like a former college linebacker, pours a cup and turns around to hand it to me.

"Welcome," he says. I accept the Styrofoam cup and thank him, wondering why he looks so familiar. I stand off to the side, hoping someone will come say hello so I don't feel so alone, but I feel like a wallflower at a high school dance, and I can feel my face redden. I wish I could pour a shot of whiskey or Irish cream into my cup, silently chiding myself for the thought. Maybe it's time to go, to put my first AA meeting in the books. I locate a trash can and toss my half-full coffee into it, then head for the door before I hear someone call my name.

"Audrey?" I turn at the sound to see the man who gave me the coffee walking over. Embarrassed that I've just thrown away the coffee he so politely handed me, I stumble over an apology. "I just realized the time and have to run. Thank you for the coffee." I take in his buzz haircut and plaid shirt with the sleeves rolled up to the elbows, and recognition suddenly sets in.

"Officer Brewer?"

He smiles. "Call me Kevin. I wasn't sure you'd remember me."

"It took me a minute, but how could I forget you? Though I suppose I'd like to, no offense. How are you?"

"I'm well," he says stiffly. "This is my favorite part of the week, even when the coffee stinks. I don't blame you for pitching it."

"It's my first meeting," I say. "But I guess you know that."

"The first one is the hardest. It gets easier, and then one day you'll wonder how you ever got by without the meetings. The weeks you can't make it will just feel wrong."

I wonder if this could ever feel normal to me, if I will ever sit through a meeting and not wish I didn't have to be here. "How long have you been coming?" I ask, as the knowledge settles on me that I am speaking to another alcoholic.

"I get my ten-year token next month," he tells me, puffing his chest out proudly.

"Wow, congratulations. That seems impossible to me right now." It's strange how comfortable I feel telling him that. If being here and standing up weren't already an admission of my problem, then that certainly is. "How hard has it been, honestly?"

Kevin sighs. "I really can't put it into words, that's how hard it is. But for you, maybe it will be easier. You've got those kids at home. How is your son, by the way? He all better?"

"He is, thank you. You know, that night . . ."

He puts a firm hand on my shoulder. "Look, that night is in the past. You screwed up, and then I did. I saw myself in you that night and how badly you wanted to fix what you'd done for the sake of your kids. I did what I had to do to give you that chance."

"What do you mean?"

"Your blood sample disappeared. Chain of custody was severed. I got too involved in something that felt close to home, and I made a decision my superior officers would have crucified me for. Then I retired."

I'm stunned at what Kevin seems to be admitting, but I can't find the words to respond.

"Your dog died, right? But your son is okay. That's what matters. You got lucky. The next time it might not work out so well. That's what you need to think about every time you think you want a drink."

"The next time already happened," I confess, feeling like I owe him my honesty in return for his. "I left my kids at home alone so I could go have a couple of drinks. While I was gone, my daughter decided to teach me a lesson." Angry, humiliated tears begin to fall. "She drank half a bottle of vodka that she'd hidden the last time." I'm sobbing now, starting to make a scene, and a few concerned people glance over. Kevin nods at them, as if to assure everyone that I'm okay. I'm clearly not the first person to break down at an AA meeting.

He exhales slowly. "Is your daughter okay?" he asks, tilting his buzz-cut head toward mine, genuinely worried.

I wipe my cheeks with the tips of my fingers and nod, and he breathes an audible sigh of relief.

"Then you got lucky twice. Think you'll get lucky three times?" he asks. I shake my head.

"There you go. *That's* your reason to never go back. You know how I said I saw myself in you? I screwed up a bunch of times, too. My wife left me and took my kids with her. I missed half their childhoods, and now they're all grown up, and I still feel like the guy who let them down when they were little. Think about that. Don't let it happen to your family."

We talk a while longer, and I leave the meeting with the knowledge that I cannot ever drink again. Not even a sip. Drinking has no place in my life anymore. Kevin put his career on the line for me, and he's right—I will not be as lucky the next time. This is going to be the hardest thing I've ever done, but Kevin gave me his cell phone number and told me to call him day or night if I needed to talk. At some point I will choose a sponsor to help guide and encourage me through this process, but in the meantime, I have him to call if I have an emergency. It's reassuring to know I've got someone on my side.

EPILOGUE

Today I am six months sober. Tomorrow I will go to my weekly meeting and pick up my chip. The chips are just symbols—tokens—but they have infinite value to me. I keep them in my jewelry box and look at them every day, and they remind me of what I've left in the past. This morning I took the five I already have out of the box and held them in my hand, feeling the weight of them. They represent the unburdening of my addiction and the milestones ahead of me. When I set them back carefully into the velvet compartment of the jewelry box, I saw my wedding rings shining up at me from inside. They, too, are a symbol of what I've put behind me.

I get home from work early today and pull my car into the driveway just in time to see the school bus arrive. Mrs. Speight is already at the curb flirting with Mr. Burns as Jacob high-fives the driver and climbs down the steps. Mrs. Speight gives Jake's cheeks a gentle squeeze, something he tolerates only from her. He is smiling today, the kind of smile that makes me involuntarily smile, too.

I catch up with them as they make their way up the path to the front door, and we continue into the house together. Jake sets his backpack on the kitchen table, and I set my laptop bag in a chair, while Mrs. Speight makes us both a snack.

I started working for a small marketing firm about a month ago. Apparently an MBA from the University of Pennsylvania is still impressive even after it has collected dust for almost fifteen years. Going back to work has been very rewarding, but it's been a tremendous challenge for me personally. I had withdrawn from people so much that now I essentially have to relearn how to be a part of a collaborative group. I'm accountable for how I spend my time and the contributions I make, and I realize that I haven't been held accountable for these things in a long time. It's been scary at times, but it's also slowly filling a space in my head and my heart that's sat empty. I work with some interesting people, most of whom are younger than I am, but who have welcomed me in a way that is warm and sincere. To them, I am Audrey Anderson, the former stay-at-home mom who decided to return to work. They ask about my kids and invite me to lunch and tell me about their own successes and failures. I have not told them about any of my greatest failures yet, but maybe one day I will.

Mrs. Speight became a part of our family after Enid came home from the hospital. She helped me in ways I still can't fully comprehend, spending time with the kids, showing me how to mother again, and becoming the mother I lost a lifetime ago. Going back to her big, empty house in the evenings became hard for her after the noise and chaos of my family all day, so when I proposed the idea of her moving in with us, she didn't have to think too hard about it. She put her house on the market, and it sold in just a couple of weeks to a sweet family with two dogs that Jacob is allowed to visit anytime he likes.

Stewart thinks having her live with us is ridiculous, but he doesn't get a say in the matter now that we've filed for divorce. It was a tough decision to make, but I suppose we had been hurting each other for so long in so many ways that in the end it made sense. We both made mistakes we couldn't forgive each other for.

Mrs. Speight is the best coparent I could ask for, and I just wish we'd been able to become close much sooner. Maybe if I'd had her as a friend and mentor sooner, I wouldn't have created such a mess, though I often wonder if we'd have needed her so much, or she us, if things hadn't happened exactly as they did.

Jacob and Nana, as Mrs. Speight is now known around here, are inseparable. They read together, draw together, and Jake cradles balls of yarn in his lap and watches with fascination when Nana sits down to knit. He's still mostly nonverbal, but he's become more flexible and content, maybe because we all are.

Enid attends a small private school now. She could never really get away from the photo that was circulated of her, and while she was taking classes online, she actually started to miss being around kids her own age, which was a good sign. She and Hannah have rekindled their friendship since one day when Hannah showed up at our door with a pint of Ben & Jerry's and two spoons.

I haven't replaced Enid's cell phone yet, which apparently cracked when she threw it at the wall after checking Instagram for the last time. She is taking a social media break, and when she wants to talk to her new friends from school, calls are made to and from our house phone. It's refreshing for now, though I have a feeling it will probably change again at some point. This is the world we live in, after all.

I talk to my sister a lot more often now. Jane left Mick and is thinking about moving to Florida, where she's found a stable looking for a new manager. We may never know the true cause of the accident that killed our parents, but my father's drinking will always be in the back of our minds, and it's something I think about every time I contemplate a drink. I know that Enid is more likely to either be an addict or marry one simply because she is my child, so I have a lot of work ahead to make sure she makes better decisions for herself than I did. I don't have to worry so much about Jake since I make most of his decisions for him, but I know they'll be better decisions than the ones I've made in the past, and I'm starting to look forward to the prospect of my forever with him.

My cell phone rings, and I smile when I see Kevin Brewer's name light up on the screen. He's coming to have dinner with us tonight and, like always, is thoughtfully checking in to see if there's anything he can pick up on the way here. Kevin diplomatically declined my request to be my AA sponsor because he felt he had already overstepped his bounds where I was concerned. To me, however, he is my saving grace, and we have become close friends. Kevin inspires me to be as successful in the pursuit of sobriety as he's been, and he hooked me up with a fantastic sponsor named Ellen. Ellen is a retired middle school teacher who now owns a coffee shop. I was shocked to find out that she was an active alcoholic during her years teaching children, but I'm reminded every day that an alcoholic can be anyone.

It's been a tough road at times for me, but Ellen is helping me see my path as a walk across the country. I start on the East Coast and make my way slowly through the overwhelming chaos of the big cities, then into the Midwest, where it will seem calm, perhaps almost manageable. Once I get to the Great Plains, I will feel like there is a wide-open expanse of nothing, and this is where she told me I'd want to drink again, to mask the aloneness and monotony I'll feel. If I can successfully navigate the Plains, I will be faced with the equivalent of the Rockies, pushing through the uphill climb and some actual physical pain until I make it to the top, when the road turns downhill and becomes easier again. The final destination will be when my journey leads me to the Pacific Ocean, a vast panorama of beauty and peace. Ellen warns me that even the majesty of my destination is wrought with hidden dangers, cliffs, and a rocky shoreline that I can fall from at any time, setting me back to the very beginning of my walk.

My walk certainly hasn't been a straight line. Sometimes I feel like I'm headed toward peace and beauty, and then all of a sudden I'm going back up those giant hills, huffing and puffing and thinking there's no way I can ever finish. I suppose that's just it—alcoholism isn't something you finish. I have to fight it every step of the way, every day that I live, but I'm willing to do it.

I'm a better mother and a better me than I used to be. I have found people to share my life with who make me want to try hard to keep going in the right direction. I have let go of the feeling that my life did not turn out quite like I once planned and have embraced the possibility that it's exactly like it was meant to be.

Kimberly Conn lives in Birmingham, Alabama with her husband and two teenage sons. *Audrey Anonymous* is her second novel.